DIARY OF A TEENAGE ZOMBIE

KRISTY BERRIDGE

Born in Perth, Western Australia in 1982, Kristy Berridge was ushered into the world in a decade of bad hair, parachute pants, and blue eye shadow. Fortunately, she managed to avoid all three influences by immersing herself in the business of growing up, and hitched a ride with her  fun-loving, and adventure-filled parents to the sunny state of Queensland. Here she completed most of her education.

Besides learning that boys *don't* have cooties, and that algebra *wouldn't* kill her, she pointedly set the path of her high school career towards success in Art and English-based subjects, and won numerous awards for her efforts.

After high school she went on to study Graphic Design and Illustration at James Cook University, and then furthered her studies at the local TAFE college with an Interior Design course. With this knowledge under her belt, she also decided to undertake a three year Design course at Rhodec International in London, to complete her education and propel her towards the successful career she now enjoys.

She currently resides in Cairns and basks in the support of friends and family who are a constant source of motivation to finish the next novel.

Shadow Ink Press
P.O Box 352n, Cairns North, Queensland 4870 Australia
Email: shadowinkpress@hotmail.com

First published in Australia 2013
This edition published 2013
Copyright © Kristy Berridge 2013
Cover design, typesetting: Chameleon Print Design

The right of Kristy Berridge to be identified as the Author of the Work has been asserted in accordance with the Copyright, Designs and Patents Act 1988.

Berridge, Kristy
Diary of a Teenage Zombie
ISBN-13: 978-0-9875247-3-7
pp228

Also by Kristy Berridge:
The Hunted
The Damned

True success comes from the fight to push forward despite the odds—this book is dedicated to all the people who tried to hold me back and failed.

A massive thank you to my number one editor, Robert Deskoski. I simply can't imagine producing a book without you now. Your insight, wisdom, and humour both educate and inspire—love your guts, Rob.

Thanks to Luke and the team at Chameleon Print Design for their brilliant cover design and typesetting work. You guys have shown bucketsful of patience, despite every one of the millions of little changes I've thrown at you.

And, of course, I also have to give a shout out to the wonderful supporters of the crowdfunding venture that helped finance this novel.

Navaro Berridge
Paul & Melissa Berridge
Sharn Swain
Stephanie & Peter Jackson
Christina Davidson
Chantelle Davidson
Dr Gavin Le Sueur
Estelle Le Sueur
Dr Grant Golombick
Dr Sami Moid
Dr Donna Usher
Kylie & Dan Thompson
Amanda Williams
Bruce Williams

CHAPTER ONE

Dear Diary,
My therapist is ~~a fucking idiot~~...

I studied the mostly blank page in front of me, the congealed ink from that erased expletive now smeared across my fingertips and making a sticky mess. I considered rubbing the excess across the front of my school jersey but knew that Mum would chuck a mental come laundry day.

That would serve her right, though. Seeing a therapist was her stupid idea, one encouraged wholeheartedly by my father, who was certain that I had more issues than the weekly gossip rag. They were blindly led by the misconception that my nail-picking, nostril-flaring therapist was a superhero with a prescription pad, destined to protect my precarious mental health, but they were wrong.

Dr Chalmers is a flame-haired geek, fixated on tinkering with my mind, like a toddler preoccupied with the possibilities of their bellybutton hidey-hole. She'd been the one to suggest this diary writing campaign, that I should probe at my thoughts and feelings, bring forth my innermost demons, and capture them in messy italic. What I suspected really fascinated the good doctor was my reluctance to talk at all.

Oh, yes. Dr Chalmers could poke and prod all she liked and try to uncover my secret—my condition—but that was something I could never allow. You see, people who discover my secret tend to get dead pretty quick.

I glanced down at the page once more, uncertain how to continue or if that was even wise. Spilling such intimate secrets where eyes could see them was plain stupid. Did I really want to be executed? Could I really leave my mum, dad and little brother Jack behind to fend for themselves?

Actually, my family would probably be better off without me. It had to be difficult for them to live with the constant threat of death—to sleep down the hall from a flippant teen who constantly violated the most basic of human rights. Who could feel safe living with a person that craved human sushi?

Confused?

The day I started looking at my little brother Jack as an appetiser I was, too. I mean, who would have thought that I, Katie Palmer—all-round socially-accepted high school sweetheart—would turn out to be one of the walking dead.

Surprise!

I don't usually run around advertising my flesh-eating nature. It makes the regular folk flip-out; I've had more than one loaded shotgun pointed in my general direction. I even had someone throw a javelin at me once. That hurt like a bitch but healed quite quickly once I ate the smirking bastard's face off. Let's just say that for a high school athletics coach, he hadn't run particularly fast at all.

But I digress. How did I become a zombie? That's a perfectly logical question, with an unfortunate answer and consequences that have changed the face of the planet. I still get mad when I think about the loss and millions of dead loved ones. That was probably why my Mum had insisted on therapy. I see her point—I'm exceedingly quick to anger now.

It had all begun with a stupid competition for the

Olympics. Popmade, the manufacturer and distributor of the most popular soda on the planet, made soft drink cheap enough for virtually anybody to afford, costing just fifty cents a throwdown. They'd promised millions of dollars to the first person who could find the lucky digits located at the bottom of one of their soda cans.

Fabulous, right?

No. Being so damn cheap, everyone started drinking this addictive, raspberry-flavoured crap, very much unaware that a serious industrial accident had occurred in the distribution factory—a secret the manufacturer kept hidden until the very first symptoms had begun to show. I'm talking about full-body deterioration and the development of flesh-eating tendencies.

Lovely.

No, it's really fucking not. At first, no one knew what the hell was going on. Here was a global phenomenon with people dropping dead, re-animating and then literally trying to have Grandma over for a barbeque. The virus spread so quickly—initially through consumption, and then afterwards through secondary bite and blood infection—it made HIV seem as harmless as the common cold.

Naturally, my parents were smart-ass vegans who eat legumes and other such rubbish, so they totally missed the boat on the undead thing. Lucky that. And Jack? Well, he was too young to drink soda at the time, so he also remained humany fresh.

We'd had an excellent security system in place and that came in handy after the epidemic first hit; that, teamed with an AK47 my dad affectionately calls 'Roger', meant that no flesh-eaters have ever crossed the threshold.

Well, except for me. But it wasn't like Dad could blow my head off like he did the neighbours across the street. Those guys used to let their miniature poodle shit all over our front lawn—Dad said they had it coming.

So, given my bitey nature and my pressing need to blend into the general, human populace, keeping a diary was probably a little more than risky. I doubted Dr Chalmers would ever get a chance to read through it, but if the information was somehow leaked by a third party, I'd be rounded up by the army and shipped to a holding facility in the desert with the rest of the decayed unliving.

Besides, I don't like the desert. It's too damn hot, sand always gets caught in my bra, and the crippling heat makes my hair look like I got dunked in a toilet.

I supposed that without a cure on the horizon there was nowhere else to put us. We stayed fresh if we fed, but if we abstained, we started to look like blistering road kill. Old Man Jack in number thirty-two was a prime example—a wheelchair-bound war veteran, we'd recently found him in a ditch by the side of the road, gaunt and with skin as rubbery as a piece of old jerky. He'd obviously had a real issue catching his meals. Dad introduced him to Roger and put him out of his misery, which was quite humane when you considered the rotting smell his flesh was inflicting on passing pedestrians.

So sticking to the basics when writing my diary entries seemed safest. Once I'd started I found that I had an awful lot to say, though most could never be uttered aloud or shared with another living soul. My family knew the truth, but my life still felt lonely, burdened and built upon deadly secrets. My parents could never truly understand. Talking about my urges, laughing when I accidentally killed the milkman … these were things I could only write on the blank page of myself.

I stopped procrastinating.

Dear Diary,

My therapist is ~~a fucking idiot~~ only trying to help, I guess.

It's hard pretending I'm normal, especially now that end of year vacation's over, and I'm headed back to school. I have to keep my guard up, remember to deodorise regularly and try not to eat ~~the special needs student's~~ hotdogs.

On another note, apparently ~~that bitch~~ Heather Rosenthal is dating Connor Watters now. I suppose I should refrain from ~~chewing off her face~~ drastic measures, despite the fact she's preying on the guy I've clearly been chasing for well over a year. I guess I'll have to think of something crafty that doesn't involve me ~~flambéing her face for breakfast,~~ getting expelled or shipped off to the desert.

I've got three months until the school formal. She's toast.

Katie xo

Okay, so that wasn't so hard. Truthfully, although clearly crossed out in black ink, the disclosure had helped to relieve some of my pent-up aggression. I could go to school today and work on a plan to nab Connor, while avoiding manslaughter.

'Katie!'

'Coming, Mum.'

I slammed the cover of my diary shut, unconcerned that I had undoubtedly smeared more stodgy ink across the page. I fingered the leather binding a moment longer, eyes searching my room for a suitable hiding place. I wasn't about to shove it under the mattress—a total cliché if ever I'd heard one. Instead, I rammed it behind my work desk, ensuring it was well and truly out of sight. I didn't want to scare Mum with my murderous transcriptions. She was already reluctant to come into my room after dark.

Satisfied, I quickly threw open my wardrobe, leafing through the clothes in an effort to find something suitably enticing. They smelt like soap and bleach, my mum being just a little on the paranoid side when it came to cleaning my school wear. I appreciated the extra layer of scent, though, as I'd rather smell like washing detergent than rotting ass.

I shirked my nightshirt and undies, quickly donning clean and fresh garments. I did a once-over in the mirror, checking for scabs, blood blisters or loose bits of skin. All was well with the undead athletics star this morning.

I'd settled on a pair of low slung jeans and a super tight t-shirt. There was no way Connor wasn't noticing me today. Team all that with a pair of matching sandals and a Gucci backpack I'd stolen from one of my dead neighbours and I was seriously styling.

'Katie!' Mum yelled for the second time.

'Yeah, I said I'm coming. Hold up!'

I'd carefully applied makeup earlier, so I was looking pale and fresh instead of my usual pasty, sallow self. My insanely long, almost black hair was a little on the lifeless side, so I'd slung it back into a ponytail to avoid closer analysis by my peers.

By the time I bounded into the kitchen, it was almost time to go. The school-sanctioned bus, with its metal grill-work and bulletproof plexiglass, generally rolled up at about eight-twenty to cart us off to school. It wasn't safe to pound the pavement any more; at least, that was what they told us. I personally thought it was an overreaction, given the fact that they hadn't caught any soccer mums trying to eat any of the local kids in over three months.

Disturbed, I stopped at the edge of the kitchen counter, fuchsia pink nails digging into the laminate surface as I studied breakfast. Mum was too busy wrangling Jack's empty porridge bowl and Dad's plate of beans into the sink to notice my discontent.

'Really, Mum?' I mumbled, studying the sturdy, stainless steel cage in front of me. A tiny ball of fluff peered back at me with beady, little eyes. 'A hamster?'

'It's the best we could do.' Dad cleared his throat and straightened his tie, a nervous tick he'd developed since the onset of my 'condition'.

'But, Dad … a hamster? I'll be starving by lunch time. Couldn't you have gotten me another cat?'

His tie now perfectly straight, Dad began to run fingers through his thicket of short, dark hair. 'The local pet store is growing suspicious. We've bought four cats from them this last month alone.'

I studied the shaking furball, wondering exactly how much nutritional value there was in a single hamster. Seriously, once you peeled back all the fur and stringy flesh you'd probably get nothing bigger than a burger patty of meat.

I sighed. My parents always tried to do their best, but this meagre offering would undoubtedly ensure a slip up in the near future. 'Thanks, Dad. I appreciate the effort.'

'We'll have to come up with a new plan. We're running out of options for food,' he murmured, now anxiously running his hands up and down the length of his thighs.

Poor Dad. The worry was slowly killing him; bags hung under his eyes and new lines were etched on his face. It was my daily reminder of the toll my habits had begun to take on this family.

As if he didn't have enough on his mind. Dad had recently been appointed Head of Zoning Sanitation. He used to be an accountant, for Christ's sake. Burying bodies in the back-yard before dawn and shovelling shit until sunset should not be what constitutes a day job.

'Leave it to me,' I said, sliding open the cage and grabbing hold of the little bundle of fluff. 'I'll think of something.'

Mum was already leading Jack away from the kitchen, making excuses and complaining that he needed to brush his crusty teeth. Naturally, Jack wanted to stay and watch his sister behead a hamster. I may have been a freak show—and a seriously bad role model—but at least I could still be entertaining.

Dad turned away as I smirked, the predator within watching the eyes of the hamster widen beyond their limits as I pushed its head into my mouth. The frantic squeaking and tiny scratching of claws against my palm were cut off in one quick bite, the sweet taste of rodent blood spilling quickly down my throat and making me groan.

I chewed swiftly and efficiently, spitting the excess fur out onto a plate that my mother had kindly provided. Dad commented on the weather and busied himself with his daily mission—locating the car keys. Mum was running around the house, yelling out for Jack to re-cap the toothpaste. Jack, though, had managed to sneak back in for the floorshow, and was kindly pointing out that a tiny foot still lingered at the corner of my mouth.

Ten minutes later Jack and I stood by the front entry, waiting for the bus to arrive. As the compression brakes hissed and the sunflower yellow painted monster rolled into view, Mum and Dad went on high alert. Anxious, they began to check the front yard, first looking through every bolted window and then tentatively sticking their heads out the front door.

Embarrassing as it was to be escorted by the parentals, I understood the necessity. It was mostly for Jack's sake, and I didn't bother to complain since it was over quickly. Plus, Dad *did* look like a total badass leading us down the driveway with Roger the AK47 in hand.

Bummer about the pink tie.

Dad ushered us quickly onto the bus, moving aside as the security grating slammed home. We were now safe inside our travelling coffin. Thankfully, my parents didn't wave. Instead, they hightailed it back to the front door and executed a well-timed commando roll as the bus pulled away from the curb. I couldn't help but shake my head at Dad's antics.

'Hey, Palmer, your fly's undone!'

I made a concerted effort not to glace down. Instead, I flashed that blonde bitch Heather Rosenthal one erect middle finger and slid into the seat beside my best mate Nikki, who was the first to applaud my not-so-eloquent retort. Jack slinked off towards the back of the bus to find solace amongst his group of primary school friends.

'Hey, chika!' Nikki wrapped an arm around my shoulder and gave me a gentle squeeze. 'Where you been all vacation?'

Trying not to eat people.

'Around,' I answered, leaning forward to tuck my backpack under the seat and evade close contact with Nikki. As it was, her nose was already flaring as if trying to weed out a bad smell. Did I double-deodorise this morning?

'You didn't even call!' she complained, though her jibing at this stage appeared good-natured. 'Your mum said something about you spending time with your grandma over the break.'

'Yeah, I haven't seen grandma in a few years and she's getting old. Dad reckons she'll kick the bucket soon.'

No, I'm not heartless, but what I was saying was mostly true. I did see grandma at the start of vacation, but she quickly figured out I wasn't the same old Katie she used to know and love—especially after she caught me trying to snatch and grab her neighbour's dog. Needless to say, a heart attack had soon followed, and her health was still touch-and-go. So, although grandma will be missed when she goes, her continued silence was a blessing.

'Wow, three months with your grandma. How boring.'

'What did you get up to?' I asked, trying to divert the conversation away from me.

'Oh, this and that. I mostly bummed around the house, bored and lonely, writing endless lists about our goals for this year.'

'Lists?' I didn't like that Nikki had bundled me into her plans. I seriously had to focus on my training, and nabbing Connor ... and, um, not eating the public.

Nikki nodded vigorously, curly red hair bouncing across her shoulders like Jell-O. 'Uh-huh. I decided that since this is our senior year, we need to exploit,' and here she paused, 'cancel that, I mean *explore* every option that's available to us on the senior calendar.'

'What exactly are we talking about here?' I said, leaning in slightly to peer at the list Nikki had grabbed from the front pocket of her backpack. 'You know that since the outbreak happened, a lot has changed. We're constantly being policed, we live on rations ... we're all in serious denial about the future.'

'All the more reason to live in the present and support the Beach Bonanza,' Nikki said, a slim finger following the messy scrawl on her overly-edited list. 'Not to mention the movie night in the park, the Winter Formal, the classroom lock-in, the—'

'Whoa, whoa,' I said, holding my hands up to curb her rising excitement. 'Did I not just mention that most of those traditions were scrapped in recent years because of the flesh-eating—'

'Zombie!' one of the boys shouted from the back of the bus.

It was like someone had set off a fire alarm during algebra;

frantic movement coupled with zealous curiosity caused all conversation in the bus to cease. The collection of eclectic age groups stuffed together, like sardines in a yellow tin can, quickly pressed their eager faces against the protective glass. As one, we scanned the deserted streets of suburbia in an effort to locate the flesh-eater.

The bus driver had already slowed the bus to avoid a collision, slapping his meaty hand over the CB radio to call in the sighting. The rest of us shrieked in horror as the blood-streaked zombie darted across the street, jumped a four foot high fence and tumbled into an unsuspecting victim's backyard.

I was surprised to see such blatant stupidity from a zombie that had survived thus far. Snacking on a friend, or Fido, in broad daylight, out in the open, was the surest way to invite capture or slaughter. Surely it would know, as did I, that Zone Security had been amped up in recent months? Or was that an irrelevant detail when one was starved and half-crazed from hunger?

Eager bursts of gunfire brought forth another collective squeal of terror. The shots were chased by an amused whooping and clapping from the senior jocks, egged on by the zombie's combat dive-and-roll back into view. Apparently the intended victim wasn't quite so unsuspecting. He was soon out in the backyard, chasing after the zombie with a double-barrel shotgun and yelling, 'So long, sucker!'

The zombie's unlife was rapidly drawing to an end, its attempts at evasion hampered by the splintered wood of the fence it was now struggling to clear. Lead was being continually pumped into his rear end. A few more rounds and this zombie would need more than a doughnut cushion to bounce back.

Everyone was clapping and cheering, and even I began to reluctantly join in, although more out of a need to maintain my camouflage than anything else. Their excitement was palpable and sickening—a good zombie killing was clearly the highlight of everyone's day.

The bus driver was soon moving us on, accelerating hard in the opposite direction. I found I felt decidedly uncomfortable knowing that the poor, hungry zombie—who now had more holes in him than a salad spinner—was destined for death. Under similar circumstances, that could have easily been me.

'That was just gross,' Nikki complained, squirming in her seat.

'It was a waste of bullets,' I muttered, settling back into my own chair. What bothered me most was the needless suffering. 'Shoot them in the head. It's the only way to take us,' and then I quickly corrected, 'I mean, them down.'

'How do you even know that?' Nikki said, scanning her list, distracted once more by the prospect of our upcoming social calendar.

I shrugged. 'YouTube.'

When our bus finally pulled up in front of the school—a wide, brick building with barred windows and heavily armed guards—my human companions all visibly relaxed. They fancied themselves safe behind those barbed-wire fences and secured entryways, with the unwavering eye of Zone Security's video surveillance always upon them.

I, on the other hand, stayed edgy, knowing that once I was behind the doors of the school I was practically a prisoner. I feared my urges, paranoid about my odour, desperate to avoid detection.

'Don't bother trying out for the cheerleading squad,' Heather said, as she laughed and shoved me out of the bus. I had to grab Nikki's shoulder to stop from ploughing face first into the pavement.

Nikki helped steady me and shot Heather a foul look.

'Why would I join the squad?' I snapped back, straightening my t-shirt and backpack. 'Don't you have to have a low IQ or something? I wouldn't want you and your minions to feel bad because I can actually spell and count past five.'

'Gee, I haven't heard that one before,' Heather replied, rolling her eyes at me and moving to block our path.

I squared my shoulders, resolute as I linked arms with Nikki and ignored the small crowd of wannabe cheerleaders that had rallied around us to support Heather. 'Just get out of our way. I can't see the door.'

'This is my school. Maybe *you* should get out of the way.'

'No, seriously,' I said, trying not to crack a smile, 'I'd need a packed lunch and directions 'cause clearly someone's been munching on the greasy food lately. I can't see past your ass, Heather, so I really need you to get the hell out of the way.'

'You bitch!' Heather shrieked, stamping her foot. 'I'm not fat!'

Nikki and I quickly slipped through the throng of laughing teens and entered the main hallway, making a hasty beeline to our lockers to avoid further conflict. We found ourselves having to duck and weave past the senior jocks as they administered their morning version of justice. They were roughing up Trenton Debrovnic, probably because he'd had the gall to actually crack open the spine of his Chemistry textbook, rather than joining in with them as they tore out the pages and made spitballs to fire at the ceiling.

'You know she's going to be a total bitch to you now,' Nikki said, looking over her shoulder, perhaps worried that Heather might be looming behind us, pom-pom nunchucks in hand.

'She pushed me out of the bus,' I answered offhandedly, cringing as the jocks began patting Trenton down, and then took his lunch tokens and dumped him headfirst into an overflowing trashcan just behind us.

'Still, making enemies with the head cheerleader and calling her fat on our first day back at school might not have been the smartest move.'

I blew her a raspberry. 'Heather's hated me since Connor asked me to train with him at the end of last semester.' Paranoid thanks to Nikki's incessant backward glances, I too began to look over my own shoulder. I could see nothing but bustling teens heading for classes and Trenton's spindly legs kicking frantically in the air. 'Besides, I don't actually think she's fat. I was just trying to piss her off.'

'Mission accomplished.'

We both snickered.

'So has marathon training started with Connor yet?'

'No, I, um,' *don't want him inhaling zombie sweat,* 'don't think he was serious. We didn't end up making plans and Connor never brought it up again, so I let it go.'

Nikki scoffed. 'Well, that just seems stupid. You could have been—'

'Hey, Palmer!'

'Speaking of,' Nikki giggled, elbowing me in the ribs. 'Now's your chance.'

As if I didn't know. With his untidy mop of dirty blonde hair, freckled nose, squared-off chin and the bluest eyes— eyes you could drown in—I'd recognise Connor Watters anywhere.

He had his backpack casually slung over one shoulder and the tiniest bundle of books imaginable wedged beneath his other arm. I saw they were football playbooks, not curriculum texts. Connor wore a faded version of our blue and gold school jersey, paired with jeans that were questionably tight—not that I minded. Like me, I was sure other schoolgirls were admiring his rear end and cared little about his future fertility.

His most entrancing feature was the wide smile currently plastered across his full lips, his flashy white teeth beaming at me. His seeming delight at bumping into me made me wonder if I was accidentally showing some nipple.

I surreptitiously glanced down at my top, satisfied that my boobs were fully covered. Naturally, paranoia urged me to covertly slip a sly finger down to the zipper of my pants, just to double-check that Heather hadn't been right about me exposing my panties.

'Hey, Palmer,' Connor repeated, now close enough that I could smell the minty freshness of his toothpaste. 'You never called me over the holidays so we could train together. Aren't you entering the marathon?'

Nikki shot me one of those *I told you so* looks before covertly kicking my ankle. My eyes watered just a little, but I managed to cover the signs of her abuse with a taut smile. 'I didn't have your number.'

Connor held an upturned palm out towards me. 'Give me your phone.'

'What?'

'Connor said to give him your phone,' Nikki prompted, kicking and elbowing me like I was ensured an immediate hook-up.

I obliged, feeling my libido slipping into overdrive. I dug into my pocket and yanked free my sparkly communication device. I mean, really, I could just as easily have been handing over the crown jewels—that's how gaudy the phone was.

Connor smirked as he slid his thumb across the touch screen and tapped in what I assumed were his details. He handed it back moments later, an eyebrow still raised as he studied its bejewelled casing. 'Now you have my number. Call me when you're going to train. I really want to kick some ass in this marathon.'

'You're assuming it's still going ahead,' I said, phone sliding back into my rear jean pocket. 'There may not have been many zombie sightings lately but they're still out there, and the organisers can't station security at every section of the track.'

'Case in point: A zombie got shot down this morning on the way to school,' Nikki pointed out, growing more animated by the second. 'You should have seen it. He practically had a bazooka shoved up his ass but still kept on going.'

'He was quite resilient,' I agreed.

'Need to shoot them in the head,' Connor said, adjusting the backpack on his shoulder.

'Why does everybody know this but me?' Nikki complained.

'YouTube,' Connor and I muttered in unison. We shared a smile, and then I glanced away, secretly awed and flattered that he was still talking to me. I'd always hoped we would, but had never expected it to happen this quickly. I checked my cleavage again.

'So, anyway,' Connor said, getting back on topic, 'call me. I don't think they'll cancel the marathon because of one zombie sighting.'

I shrugged, not nearly as confident.

'Besides, the marathon gives each of the Zones something to look forward to.'

'You mean, gives the bookies something to bet on.'

A teasing smile touched the corners of Connor's lips. 'This event promotes good health, too, and is a great reminder that training to run far and fast these days is more than just beneficial—it's lifesaving.'

'That it is,' I coughed, trying to contain the laughter that threatened to burst forth. I kept imagining a race between the overweight townsfolk, senior citizens, and me. Up against my unbeatable gait there really was no competition, only snack breaks along the way.

Connor bobbed his head. 'So I guess I'll see you later, then?'

'Yeah, um, later.'

He flashed me with another megawatt smile and waved. That perfectly-formed ass, snug inside those tight jeans, sauntered off down the corridor, the crowd of mixed seniors and juniors parting in his wake as if he owned the place. Shamefully, Nikki and I just stared.

'I don't know how that boy ever made it through puberty,' Nikki commented, neck tilting ninety degrees. 'Are you seeing how tight those pants are?'

'I know, right?'

We were giggling, watching until the very last minute as Connor disappeared around the corner, and then Nikki was shoving me towards our lockers. 'Come on, show's over.'

I slammed a fist against the stubborn metal of my locker door, knowing that a cheap shot to the right-hand corner usually made it spring right open.

The main problem with being extra strong? I often forget about it until someone's unconscious or there's a brand new hole in the dining room table. 'Fuck,' I muttered under my breath, observing the rather large new dent in the metalwork with dismay.

'Christ, Katie. What did your locker ever do to you?' Thankfully, Nikki was just teasing.

I laughed along with her, relieved as Nikki focused on grabbing her own books for class. I hefted a few I'd need for first period into my backpack and attempted to re-close the locker. Unfortunately, now the metal catch wouldn't close and was left swinging open.

'Looks like you'll need a padlock now. We wouldn't want the teachers finding your stash of black market porn,' Nikki joked, as she slammed her unmarked locker door home.

'I was more concerned about the illegal firearms.'

The moment of shared humour soon passed as we contemplated the day ahead. 'So, what have you got first up?'

'Home Economics.'

Nikki clapped her hands, as excited as ever. 'I love that class.'

I fucking hated Home Economics. Since becoming a zombie, the smell of human food tended to sicken me. I'd tried to drop the class before the start of semester but no dice; the Vice Principal hadn't believed that I was gluten, dairy, wheat, seafood, nut, and soy intolerant.

'I guess I'll see you after?' I said, mirroring the retreating footsteps of all the other students traversing the hallways to class.

'For sure.' Nikki gave a quick wave and headed in the opposite direction.

Class was already filling up by the time I slipped through the door. There weren't a whole lot of people here from my social circle, mostly because the school mixed different grades into each class. I slid easily into a chair beside some other track and field athletes.

Chatter was kept to a minimum, and as if on autopilot, we pulled out the recommended reading material and settled into our stiff-backed plastic chairs. Flipping through the pages seemed like good preparation, but as I studied the photographs and waited for the teacher to arrive, I contemplated excusing myself due to sudden illness.

The aptly-named Mrs Cook appeared in a hailstorm

of polka dots, frills and blood red lipstick, her long, slim fingers already reaching for a stick of chalk. She began to elegantly scribe her name upon the blackboard, despite everyone already knowing exactly who she was. I suspected she got a kick out of reminding us she was in charge.

'I trust you all had a pleasant vacation?' she asked, dusting her chalky fingers across the front of her skirt. 'I'm Mrs Cook, for those of you who are unaware. Now, have you all been studying the required reading material during the break?'

A chorus of groans and meagre protests erupted. It was painfully obvious that no one had cracked open their cookery book before entering the classroom today.

'Well I suppose that settles it,' she grumbled, reaching for her teacher's copy of the textbook. 'Turn to page thirty-two, the chapter entitled *Knife Skills* in the text. I noticed that after last semester, despite some quite delicious dishes from a few of you, your cutting and dicing left a lot to be desired. So, in light of this fact, head to your benches and look at what I have nestled in your fridges.'

Steel legs scraped across the chipped linoleum, the perfect accompaniment to the other students' ongoing groans of protest. I, on the other hand, was curious—when you're being chased by an angry mob, knife skills could come in handy ... for avoiding further conflict, of course.

I wandered to the back of the classroom, quickly nabbing the same tiny kitchenette I'd been allocated the previous year. A shady truth, and probably a misconception, but hiding at the back of the room usually equated to invisibility among my peers.

I peered inside the mini refrigerator, pleased to see a plate of raw meat and vegetables wedged snugly in the chiller. As a member of the living dead, I generally needed to eat fresh, bloody meat to keep functioning. This meat wasn't exactly kicking and begging for life, but a rump steak, boneless chicken and fresh fish didn't exactly offend.

Mrs Cook clapped her hands to silence the room and then placed them on her hips, now weaving in and out between benches as she observed each of us in turn. 'We are going to start by practising the *Julienne*. Begin.'

The rest of the class soon faded into a chopping blur, and before I knew it I was on my way to Algebra. Nikki was saving me a seat in her own unique way—reclining dangerously on the tottering legs of her graffiti-ridden chair and dangling her ankles over the edge of the desk beside her. Her head was buried in some tawdry romance novel, her lower lip sucked between her teeth.

Fabio's quivering member was clearly a hit.

I pushed her legs off the edge of my desk, catching her left ankle before her chair tipped completely backwards and took her and the desk with it. 'Fuck *me*, Katie,' she grumbled, righting herself, the book still in hand. 'You nearly knocked me off my chair!'

'Learn anything new?' I said, gesturing to the novel she still had clasped tightly between her fingers.

Nikki's filthy look only served to make me smile. 'I was just getting to the good stuff before you interrupted.'

'What good stuff? You know those highlanders and sexy sea pirates don't actually have seven inch coc—'

Nikki quickly interrupted. 'Shut your mouth before you ruin all my illusions. Although … if I have to read the word "throbbing" one more time, I'm going to lose my shit.'

'Want some of my black market porn?'

'Shut up.'

'Then stop reading that crap,' I teased, taking the chair beside her.

All joking ceased as Heather entered the room, moving

to take a seat at the front of the class with the rest of her devoted cronies. Naturally, all the rambunctious boys stopped to admire her double-D counterparts; all the other girls in the room stopped to glance, envious of her elfin good looks.

Even I had to concede that Heather would look breathtaking, the sun beating down upon her golden skin, as the school bus repeatedly backed over her contorted limbs.

'So, are you going to call Connor?' Nikki asked, redirecting my attention.

'We only talked an hour ago.'

Nikki blew a rather loud raspberry, and then immediately ducked for cover as the cold and calculating gaze of the pencil-thin Mr Gray—algebra teacher extraordinaire—entered the room. As he barked at us to open our textbooks, Nikki leaned towards me conspiratorially, lowering her voice. 'If you're training this afternoon, you should invite Connor to join you.'

'Can't,' I stated matter-of-factly. 'I have an appointment.'

'With who?'

My therapist.

'Katie. Nikki. Would you like to share your conversation with the rest of the class?'

Clearly, we did not.

* * *

The rest of the day stayed pretty much how it started—relatively uneventful. That wasn't counting the zombie showdown in suburbia or the morning's verbal thrashing with Heather. I certainly wasn't going to count my brief encounter with Connor either, mostly because I was still in awe of the attention. I mean, if he was dating blonde-haired, big-boobed Heather, then this begged the question: What the hell did he want with me?

'Hello, darling,' Mum cooed as I slid into our rusting station wagon, with its cracked leather seats and busted up dashboard. The flashing neon clock said she was twenty minutes late, but I trusted its accuracy as much as I trusted the car's thinning brake pads.

'Hi,' I responded, slinging my backpack over my shoulder and onto the backseat.

'Hey!' Jack protested, rubbing at his forehead. He shoved my bag onto the floor.

'Sorry, bud,' I murmured, offering a reassuring smile. 'I thought you'd be catching the bus home.' As a wet, pointy tongue emerged, aimed in my direction, I frowned and focused back on Mum.

Kids.

'Do I have to see Dr Chalmers this afternoon?'

Her wry expression suggested that I did.

'Come on, Mum. We both know she can't help me. If anything, Chalmers could get me into a lot of trouble.'

'Well, you could always eat her if she starts to suspect.'

Jack screeched from the backseat. 'Yuck!'

'Uncalled for,' I chided, poking her in the shoulder.

'Okay, okay,' Mum continued, hands leaving the steering wheel in a brief show of surrender. 'You know I'd never encourage that sort of behaviour.'

'Just as well. I was starting to think that you might be in need of some serious couch time yourself … you freaking sadist.'

Mum giggled and then cleared her throat, suddenly an adult again. Quickly assessing her blind spot before signalling, we were soon leaving the school car park behind in the rear-view mirror. 'Well, since you don't think you need therapy, why don't we try some word association?'

'Mum, watching re-runs of Dr Phil does not make you a qualified psychologist.'

'You want to know why you have to see Dr Chalmers?'

'Because I'm trapped in the car with an enabler?'

She slapped playfully at my arm. 'What's the first thing that comes to mind when I say the word "family"?'

'Dinner,' I blurted, quickly clamping a hand over my traitorous lips.

'There you have it,' Mum wisely answered, though not nearly as glib now as she had been with her earlier teasing. 'You have to see Dr Chalmers so I don't have to lock you outside the house.'

Jack was now incessantly tapping Mum's shoulder, waiting for her to acknowledge his annoying presence. 'Mum? Mum? Mum! Mum?'

'Yes, Jack!' she bellowed, swatting his hand away and fixing narrowed eyes back on the road.

Jack eyed me suspiciously, sliding to the other side of the vehicle and out of immediate reach. 'Is Katie really going to eat us?'

'Only if you don't stay out of my room.'

'Katie!'

'What? We're running out of hamsters.'

* * *

Dr Chalmers's office was on the outskirts of town, tucked into one of the supposed safe districts. Zone Three was a cardboard cut out of suburbia, cordoned off with barbed wire fences and regular security patrols. The block comprised a local market, movie theatre, outlet mall and small commercial district, all crammed together for convenience and safety.

Mum sat idle, her eyes on the lowered boom gate ahead.

Security guards were running their usual checks on the vehicles entering the district, just to make sure we didn't have a zombie stashed in the boot—or, you know, in the front passenger seat.

Mum drummed her fingers incessantly on the steering wheel, smiling brightly as one of the patrolman tapped on the side window. I knew the signs—she was nervous, a layer of perspiration already beaded on her forehead. There was a distinct possibility of hyena laughter and rapid eye twitching on the near horizon.

'Keep it together, Mum.'

'You keep it together!' she snapped, winding down the window.

'Afternoon,' the patrolman drawled, his portly belly spilling in over the rubber seals of the open window. I was suddenly mesmerised by the strained, mint green fabric of his uniform, uncertain how Mum could stand being mere inches from the Lost World of Belly Button Lint and not throw a gold coin into the abyss, wink, and make a wish.

'Afternoon, officer.'

'Just the three of you?' he asked, ducking down to peer at Jack and me. Jack kindly showed him some tongue, while I kept staring into that linty peephole. I was certain now that black holes existed. If I moved even an inch, I'd get sucked right into this one.

'Yes,' Mum answered stiffly.

'Can you pop the boot for me, please?'

'Certainly.'

After five minutes of digging through the charity bag clothes we'd never delivered to the collection bins, questioning Jack on the contents of his lunch box, and examining my low, sensible heels, Mr Belly Lint let us pass into the Zone. I still wasn't clear how a brief car inspection was classified as a decent security check, but I figured if security didn't give a shit about letting me in, then neither should I.

'Do you want us to come in with you?' Mum asked, as she locked the car behind us.

I shook my head. 'Nah, just come back and get me in an hour.'

Mum and Jack left me on the sidewalk outside Dr Chalmer's office. Jack was begging Mum to take him to the games arcade as they walked off, yanking on her shirt tails to press home his point. As they disappeared around a corner, I could just hear Mum as she started to play more word association games, making it clear that 'technology' and 'fun' equated to 'aneurisms' and 'square-eyes'.

Meanwhile, I took in the weathered door that led to the good doctor's office—a handwritten sign had been hastily tacked with mismatched drawing pins to its surface, indicating the business within. This, combined with the graffiti strewn across the building's exterior, and along with the scent of urine in the air, made me wonder just exactly how Mum had come across the good Dr Chalmers.

The door creaked as I opened it, the dulcet tones of classical music emanating from within. It did little to soothe my apprehension and even less to add appeal to what was the shabbiest of entry halls.

Two beige armchairs sat to the right of the door, an array of pre-zombie gossip magazines neatly arranged on a chipped, melamine side-table. Stained carpet ran underfoot, leading like an arrow to Dr Chalmers's office door. Nonsensical images lined the walls in a mockery of any decent attempt at decorating.

The music stopped as I closed the door behind me. Dr Chalmers emerged at the end of the hall, a wide smile on her face. 'Katie,' she beamed, as warm and welcoming as ever, 'won't you come in?'

I nodded, slipping my thumbs into the pocket of my jeans and traipsed begrudgingly up the soiled carpet. She closed the door behind us and gestured for me to take a seat. Hers wasn't one of those comfortable recliners you see in the movies, but more a wooden-backed dining chair. I suspected Dr Chalmers was a cheap bitch who'd never heard of IKEA.

'So, Katie,' the doctor murmured, settling into her cushioned armchair and retrieving her notepad, 'what would you like to talk about today?'

I shrugged, my eyes wandering around the room's dingy interior. Honestly, it was no better than the outside hallway. Oh, wait, there was a sleek, silver lamp with a busted bulb on her desk and a wax potted plant covered in dust. I supposed that was something.

'How was school?' Dr Chalmers asked, already making notes, though of what I had no idea.

'Same old.'

'Did you make any new friends?'

'I'm a senior. I already know everyone.'

'Of course,' Dr Chalmers agreed. 'What about your classes?'

'What about them?' I fidgeted, uncomfortable with the very concept of therapy. Why would you pay someone to probe and expose your innermost thoughts, only to tell you that you have daddy issues? What a fucking waste of time and money.

'Are you enjoying anything in particular in your classes?'

'I learnt some knife skills today.'

Perhaps intrigued, she peered over the edge of her wire-rimmed glasses. 'Sounds interesting.'

I answered with another shrug.

'And what would you need knife skills for?'

'Gutting the walking dead.'

An eyebrow rose to spectacular heights. 'They're teaching that in school now?' The doctor shifted in her seat, crossing one slender leg over the other. 'My, my. A lot has changed since my day.'

I scoffed, positive everything had changed since the early 1800's. In her day people hadn't lived in security controlled Zones to prevent the hostile takeover of flesh-eating zombies. Similarly, we also didn't wear petticoats and hooped skirts anymore. 'Sorry. Bad joke. I just meant that I practised how to *julienne* carrots in Home Economics today.'

Dr Chalmers's sigh of relief was marked by a frown, perhaps more ruffled by my warped sense of humour than she'd let on. Last session, she'd made it clear that my toilet humour was an obvious deflection. Personally, I think I'm just juvenile—number ones and twos are funny.

'What other school-based activities are you enjoying?'

So we were back on track again. 'Well, my friend Nikki's trying to get me involved in a few events this year but it's only the first day and Connor Wat ... never mind.'

Dr Chalmers cocked her head to one side, pressing her slipping frames up the bridge of her nose. Her eyes were once again observing me critically. 'Who is Connor?'

Bugger. 'Just this guy who wants to train with me for the marathon.'

'You've never mentioned boys or a marathon before.'

'This is only my second session,' I reminded her.

'Tell me more about the boy.'

'Why?'

She made some notes on her pad. 'Fine. Tell me about the marathon, instead. I didn't realise you were athletic.'

I offered a reluctant smile; I really couldn't help it. I was a track and field star, or at least I had been before the world went to shit and my dreams of participating in the Olympic Games had blown apart. Now I just tried to stay fit and healthy, prepared in case one day they reinstated sporting events—like the local Zone marathon. 'Truthfully, given the current circumstances I have no idea if the marathon will go ahead.'

'You're referring to the zombie sighting in Zone Two this morning?'

I was taken aback, my fingers gripping the underside of the stiff chair. 'How do you know about that already?'

Dr Chalmers consulted her notes briefly before looking up, fingers eagerly tucking a stray lock of auburn hair behind one ear. 'A bulletin was posted, Katie. The walking dead *are* still among us.' Her pointed gaze lingered on me longer than I felt comfortable with. 'Running a marathon right now probably isn't the wisest decision. After all, people are being killed every day.'

I cringed. 'So the neighbour with the shotgun, the guy who blew the zombie's rear end to bits, died this morning?'

She seemed momentarily confused. 'I was referring to the night clerk at the food mart. Who are you talking about?'

'Holy shit! Mr Chan is dead?'

Dr Chalmers placed her notepad and pen on top of her desk, and clasped her hands on the end of her knee. 'I apologise, Katie. This was not how I intended the session to end, with us talking about someone else. May I ask instead how the journal writing is going?'

Seriously? She was asking me about my diary when the guy who'd made the best dim sum in town had just been chewed out by the undead? This was a tragedy of epic proportions.

'Katie?' the doctor prompted.

'I'm not sure if I'm totally comfortable with it. I don't know what to write,' I said, rubbing my sweaty palms up and down the length of my thighs.

'Every urge, desire and transgression—it's important for you to expel what you keep hidden within. Writing it all down is just another form of therapy, or an outlet, if you will.'

'I don't need an outlet. I have nothing to say.'

'We all have secrets, Katie.'

I narrowed my eyes, instantly suspect. 'How can you be sure?'

She pursed her glossed lips, fingers drumming ever so lightly on the end of her knees. 'Do you really have to ask?'

We left it at that, our session ending on an unsettling note. I wasn't really sure what she'd meant by her last statement, but I suspected Dr Chalmers was slightly smarter than she'd first appeared. I'd have to be more careful than ever or seriously start thinking about taking Mum up on her earlier suggestion.

CHAPTER TWO

Dear Diary,

I found a tiny padlock on Jack's bedroom door last night. I suspect Mum and Dad are a little worried about my ~~flesh eating tendencies~~ bad temper. They must have found bits of the Nelson's cat in our backyard.

But my complexion looks awesome today and that's a good thing, because Connor called me yesterday and organised a ~~date~~ training session for this morning. I couldn't exactly think of a reason not to, since my armpits smelled okay and Mum had double-washed my jogging gear in preparation.

Bless her.

I'm also going to meet up with Nikki after classes this morning to organise the classroom lock-in, the first stop on our social calendar for the year. Right now I think it's a great idea, but I'm ~~well fed~~ in a good mood. Who knows how I'll feel at the end of the week ~~when my skin starts peeling away from my face?~~

Katie xo

Connor was already waiting for me on the back oval by the time Mum dropped me off at school. Being awake at such an ungodly hour meant I was still yawning, scratching at my belly and rubbing pockets of dried sleep from the corners of my eyes.

I know. I paint a pretty picture of myself. I'd have rather worn a low-cut top and slapped on some make-up, but it was only just after six and running a few miles would make me sweat like a pig. Practicality was key.

'Palmer,' Connor greeted me, a broad smile plastered across his face. 'I'm not keeping you up, am I?'

'I usually train in the afternoon,' I complained, covering my mouth as another yawn threatened to escape. Suddenly my tired brain remembered that this was the hottest guy in school and that this morning he'd woken up especially early to go running with me. I quickly changed my attitude.

Happy dance.

'Boo-hoo,' he teased, blonde hair flopping in front of his eyes. Connor smoothed his fringe back from his forehead and continued to reach up with the one motion, stretching his arms high above his head.

'Let's just hope you can keep up.'

Small wonder that I found the words at all given my current distraction. A quick glimpse at Connor's toned abdominals and exposed Calvin Klein briefs and my imagination was overflowing with unladylike, erotic thoughts.

'Is that a challenge, Palmer?'

'Take it however you want.' I shook my head in an effort to break the spell his underwear apparently held over me. Languid scenes of our sweaty flesh pressing together stirred my desire, threatening to weaken me at the knees.

Connor's knowing grin suggested he was more than aware of my eyes on him, plotting the possibilities.

Fuck.

Embarrassed by my open gaze, I sniffed and rolled my shoulders, reaching back to grip an ankle and stretch out my quadriceps, and then hamstrings and calves. I didn't need the preparation but I wanted to look anywhere but at

Connor, certain there was a flashing neon sign above my head that screamed 'desperate'.

'You ready?' Connor asked, patting me on the back.

Was it wrong to savour that casual touch? I decided to embellish upon it in my fantasies later on. As far as I was concerned, that innocent gesture would be re-counted instead as brazen fingers grazing my spine, warm palms flattening against me and sliding down my back until they were cupping my ass. Connor would tell me he could crack walnuts on it.

Yes. That would be how I'd inaccurately remember this moment.

I took a deep breath, inconspicuously sniffed at my armpits, and then nodded. Connor had already bolted from the starting plate with a hiss and a roar, setting an unsustainable pace in his eagerness to impress. Several laps at this speed would undoubtedly lead to him coughing up a lung—an oxygen tank loomed in his foreseeable future.

After circling the track a few dozen times and hitting our five-kilometre unspoken goal, I slowly realised that Connor was not built for endurance. Keeping pace with his frenetic stride was almost too easy, yet he struggled on and tried to match my predatory gait. Sweat trickled down Connor's face and saturated his shirt. He was puffing like a geriatric chasing a big-breasted blonde; his face was rose-tinted, and his blue eyes were bulging.

'Palmer!' he gasped. 'What kind of stride do you call that?'

'The one you set?' I felt a little bad. My breathing was easy, and I had just lapped him for the second time in five minutes. Nikki had made it clear that in order to win Connor's affections I had to embrace my athleticism but also not show him up. Something about damaging his ego, which she'd likened to kicking him in the balls.

'You're not jogging, you're running!' Connor panted. He was tripping over his own feet, his arms windmilling to keep himself upright.

My inner predator rolled her eyes as I slowed, fighting to contain a hysterical outburst. 'I'm sorry. Do you need a rest?'

Connor was well behind me now. He had regained his balance but was swaying, perhaps on the verge of passing out. Bent in half and with hands propped against his knees, he attempted to draw in great gasps of air, but instead started to cough like he'd contracted emphysema.

I doubled back, concerned by the sudden paleness of his skin. 'Are you okay?' I asked, tentatively smoothing my hand across his back. The muscles bunched and tightened under my palm, but Connor was inconsolable, shoving me out of the way. Seconds later he was emptying the contents of his stomach onto the field.

'Wow,' I yelped, jumping free of the partially-digested debris, 'I guess we know who's going to win this upcoming marathon, huh?'

The contemptuous glare Connor shot me as he wiped his mouth suggested I was doing less than my best to lure him in with my feminine wiles.

Fuck.

* * *

'So what are we protesting this year?' I asked Nikki, as she tapped away at the keyboard in front of her. I closed the door to the computer room behind me, satisfied we wouldn't be bothered by the prying eyes of other students as the lock clicked shut.

'Take your pick,' she murmured, barely registering my arrival.

'We've only been back at school for a few days. What could the student body possibly have to complain about that warrants a lock-in?'

'It's tradition, so the why doesn't really matter. It's just a great bonding experience for the seniors.'

Unconvinced, I approached the table where she was sitting and peered over Nikki's shoulder. 'Whatcha doing?'

'Checking Facebook.'

I rolled my eyes. I was blown away that social networking was still prioritised amongst my peers. Of course, nothing could kill the Internet—not even the zombie apocalypse— but apparently liking the statuses of a guy who'd mastered the art of pole-dancing in a mankini, as well as commenting on all the idiots posting 'selfies', was still publically embraced.

Nikki continued to read quietly to herself, clicking several posts before slumping back in her chair. Her features twisted in disbelief. 'Mr Chan is dead.'

I squeezed her shoulder gently. 'Oh yeah, I'm sorry. I found out about that yesterday but forgot to tell you. It's sad, isn't it?'

'There's a Facebook page dedicated to his passing. Apparently, he died from a zombie attack.'

'Well, duh. Does anyone actually die of natural causes anymore?' I muttered, rolling my eyes.

Nikki slapped the hand I had resting on her shoulder. 'Don't be an insensitive dick. He made awesome dim sum.'

I settled into the chair next to her, throwing my backpack onto the floor by our feet. 'Not to piss you off further with my apparent insensitivity, but are we organising this lock-in thing, or what? I've got places to be this afternoon.'

Clearly, Nikki was still distracted by the memorial page in front of her. I was surprised that Mr Chan had enough fans left to put one up, especially since most of the town had lost family and friends during the initial outbreak. I was clearly underestimating the call of the wonton.

'That's two attempted zombie attacks in the last few days, one of them successful,' Nikki commented, her fingers still tapping away at the keys as she left a comment offering her condolences. 'I thought there weren't many left.'

'What? Zombies?' I blew a raspberry. 'Come on. This is a worldwide epidemic that won't be over until they find a cure. In the meantime, we can't afford to be complacent. Mr Chan is a prime example.'

'He was in a safe Zone.'

'There's no such thing. It's all just an illusion, Nikki. If the zombies want in, they get in.'

Nikki frowned. 'Do you think it's still safe to go ahead with the lock-in?'

I pondered the question, surreptitiously rubbing at my stomach. As long as no one outed me and I'd fed before being padlocked in with the other seniors, all would be well. 'This school is one of the most secure places in town. I doubt we have anything to worry about.'

She nodded her agreement, and then suddenly spun in her seat, knees bouncing up and down excitedly. 'Ooh! What happened with Connor at training this morning?'

The abrupt change in subject was jarring. I found myself frowning, but then remembered Connor's roaming hand—the way it touched my back, stroked my hips, tickled my stomach and curved around to embrace my eager behind. Oh, yes, embellishing those events had been awesome. Recollection soon poured icy water all over my burning libido as chunks of regurgitated corn swam into my inner field of vision. 'Um, what?'

'Connor. You. This morning. Give me the deets!'

'Well, he's seriously unfit,' I joked, reclining comfortably in my chair. 'A five kilometre run had him upending breakfast.'

'Really? He's one of the best athletes at school.'

I pulled my long, dark hair over my shoulder and started picking at the ends. 'Clearly not. I totally kicked his ass.'

Nikki slapped a hand against her forehead, groaning like she was giving birth to a watermelon. 'Katie, why would you do that? What did I tell you?'

I shrugged, not willing to admit to anything incriminating.

'You showed him up, didn't you?'

'What was I supposed to do?'

'Make him look good.'

'But that would have been impossible!'

Nikki was shaking her head. 'Katie, Katie, Katie. You've dated enough of the idiots in this school to know how their minds work.'

I scoffed. 'Making out with a few drunken guys at the Beach Bonanza does not count as dating.'

Suddenly pensive, Nikki rocked back on the rear legs of her chair, smoothing a loose curl into place as she studied my expression.

'What? All this staring you're doing is killing me.'

Nikki narrowed her eyes, only serving to intimidate me further. 'Do you think Connor will ever want to train with you again?'

'I seriously doubt it. I really screwed up.'

'Anything redeemable?'

'He got to see my boobs bouncing around. Does that count?'

'Were you wearing a bra?'

'I'd be suffering facial injuries if I wasn't.'

'They aren't that big,' Nikki jeered, looking me up-and-down.

'Ooh, burn!' I answered, slapping a hand to my heart in a gesture of mock grief.

Nikki stopped swinging on her chair, slamming back against the floor with a hiss of frustration. She looked like one of those dashboard dog bobble-heads, as she began shaking her head again, logging out of the Internet and shutting down the computer.

Muttering under her breath how hopeless I was, she pulled out a notepad and pen from her backpack, taking the time to date the page and add additional notes. She began to divide the page into two sections, one titled *Katie's Love Life* and the other *Senior Lock-in*. I grew concerned, wondered if she was planning on combining the two, which was both disturbing and interesting, though.

'Um, what are you doing?'

'Isn't it obvious?' Nikki muttered, green eyes almost glowing with enthusiasm. 'I'm trying to get you laid.'

CHAPTER THREE

Dear Diary,

There's been another attack ~~and for once it wasn't me. In fact, I haven't eaten in days~~. Everyone at school is talking about it, and most people reckon the lock-in might not be going ahead tonight.

Secretly I'm relieved that I may not have to go. ~~The pet store is a no go and Dad has forbidden me from hunting nearby. Apparently my methods are sloppy, and he's still going on about the bones in the mulch pile.~~

There's been progress on the Connor front, despite the earlier blows to his ego. He said he still wants to meet up with me every morning for training and apologised, explaining that a bout of the flu impeded his last efforts. I've declined for the last few days on account of my sub-par personal hygiene, but he's still interested!

Heather's still being a nasty bitch. She snapped a photo of one of my bigger facial pustules and posted it on Facebook, tagging it as the 'world's biggest pit of pus'.

I've seriously considered kicking her in the you-know-what, but Nikki reminded me that fanny fighting's not a real sport.

~~OMG, I'm so hungry! I wonder if that homeless guy that lives on the outskirts of Zone Two is still around?~~

Laters,

Katie xo

I crept through the darkness of the underpass spanning Zone Two and Three, the sounds of the river lapping at the sandy shore close by a welcome companion. A few random cars occasionally passed overhead, the rhythm of the tyres thumping over slight divots in the bitumen almost hypnotic.

Venturing out after dark was extremely rare. Most people locked themselves up tight at dusk—floodlights illuminated front and rear yards and shotguns within easy reach. Creeping like a thief in the night? That was totally unheard of, but I didn't have anything but the living to fear anymore.

I ventured further into the dark, following the scent of unwashed skin and cheap bourbon. I was so hungry, so desperate for flesh and the sweet taste of blood that I'd snuck out of the house. Mum and Dad must have assumed I was still beautifying for the lock-in, but how they thought I could conceal a peeling chin, oozing scabs at the hairline and rheumy eyes I had no idea. I closely resembled that dead chick *Corpse Bride* but on crack.

And Revlon could only fix so much.

A throaty groan, followed by a phlegm-filled cough, signalled that I was homing in on the homeless guy's location. I'd seen him wandering aimlessly around the mall in Zone Three about two weeks previously. After the latest spate of attacks, it was amazing Mr Drunky was still alive considering the many flesh-eaters in our midst.

Well, his number was up. I was starving and smelt like leaky sewerage; stray cats and small rodents were not going to cut it after two weeks without 'food'.

I snapped to attention, my senses on high alert as I heard a strangled gasp and the sickening *thud* of a body being tossed aside. The cloying scent of blood marred the air, the liquid wheezing of a man drowning in his own fluids an invitation I suddenly could not refuse.

I surrendered stealth for speed, closing in quickly on the barely-visible form huddled by the base of the overpass pylons. That hulking mass was too great to be a single individual, so I slowed my advance. Was that another of my kind?

Compelled by murderous instinct and driven by unsated hunger, I drank in the mouth-watering scent of gouged flesh, the slickness of blood-coated insides practically shimmering in the moonlight like unearthed gold.

My legs moved of their own volition, thumping the compact soil underfoot and propelling me towards the competition. A hiss escaped my lips, the hunger within filling my inner predator with need. This was my town—this was my drunken bum.

I didn't see the zombie's face as it turned heel and ran, but I felt its uncertainty slither through me. Doubt was a sudden and unwanted notion.

I shook off the unease as I inspected the recently deceased. Vital liquids and internal organs were spewing out on the ground like discarded party poppers. Sloppy seconds was a concept I was more than comfortable with, the burning ache of desperate hunger overriding my better judgement.

A few more steps brought me just alongside the body, my fingers twitching at my sides like a junkie in desperate need of a fix. I refrained from diving head first into the entrails, trying in vain to keep a cool head as I once again scanned the darkness beyond for signs of movement or further competition.

My fleeting inspection of the surrounding landscape was just that ... fleeting. I'd heard of Zone Security setting up traps not dissimilar to this, yet that risk didn't seem to quell my desire to feed.

Anyway, I won't bore you with all the gory details. I threw caution to the wind and stripped that guy like an abandoned car in the ghetto. Afterwards, all that remained was a pile of bones and his wrinkly, old pecker.

By the time I returned home it was well after nine. The lock-in, if it had proceeded, was undoubtedly already in progress and Nikki would be fuming, wondering why I wasn't there to co-host. I had other worries, though. My backside would be smarting for days after my parents finished dishing out the punishment I'd earned from this little escapade.

'Katie!' Dad barked as he threw open the front door, grabbing me by the collar of my shirt and quickly dragging me inside. 'Have you seen yourself?'

'Um ...' I could only look at myself from the chest down, and even I had to admit I totally should have used a bib. Shit, was that a bit of eyeball stuck in my cleavage?

'Katie!' It was Mum's turn to shout. 'What have you done!?'

'I was hungry,' I grumbled, twisting my blood-slicked fingers in front of me. I had to admit that this looked pretty bad. I looked like a pig in mud, covered in my own fifth. 'I'm sorry.'

'You're sorry?' Dad yelled, and I knew this was only the start of my troubles. 'Katie, with the recent sightings it's not safe for you to leave the house at night, especially not looking like this. My God, you know how trigger happy we all are since the outbreak!'

'Dad, I know. Believe me, I'm sorry, but you really don't understand.'

'You know I would have found something for you. I would have driven all night until we found you food.'

Mum's eyes were fixed on the drying blood enmeshed in the fibres of my shirt and jeans. 'What sort of blood is that?' Her voice, devoid of any anger, was now barely a whisper. I could practically smell the fear radiating out from her pores.

'Um ...'

'Oh my God,' she moaned, falling to her knees in all manner of amateur dramatics. 'Did you kill Mr Chan?'

'What, tonight?'

Dad slapped me on the back of my head. I guess I deserved it. I was making light of another's death in lieu of softening the blow for my own current murder. Yep, that didn't make any sense to me either, so I knew I was definitely being a shit.

'No, of course I didn't kill Mr Chan.'

'Then the blood?'

'A really, really big cat.'

That earned me a second slap, a little harder than the previous one.

'Okay, I'm sorry. It wasn't a cat. It was the homeless guy who lives under the underpass.'

My parents groaned in unison, their faces entirely drained of blood, pastier than my latest kill. 'What are we going to do about this?' Dad asked, of no one in particular.

'There isn't much left,' I added helpfully. 'I doubt very much if anyone will find him for a while.'

'Go to your room,' Mum growled, pointing to the stairs.

'I'm so sorry, guys. You know I would never do this if I wasn't left without a choice, right? I was falling apart and the lock-in—'

'You think you're going to the lock-in now?'

'Well, I'm not all oozy anymore,' I reasoned, smoothing my fingers over clear skin.

'Katie, go to your room!'

I obliged without further discussion. I mean, I really hadn't wanted to go to the lock-in anyway, but now I was on a food high and my skin was as smooth as a baby's hind-quarters. It seemed a waste.

Instead of heading straight to my room, I detoured, prefer-ring to spend some alone time in the bathroom. Looking in the mirror, I was confronted by the true horror of my crime.

I'd killed people before, sadly, and probably quite a

few—women and children included. It started with that rotten kid from Zone Five who used to call me the Blair Bitch Project; after that, by an unsupportive athletics coach who had a penchant for throwing spears.

Don't ask.

Anyway, studying my reflection, I thought perhaps I'd feel a slight pang of remorse. Where was the burrowing self-resentment that would make me question my motives, the lingering hint of humanity? Instead there was nothing but the satisfied gurgling of a full stomach. I was a murderous schmuck—a *bloated*, murderous schmuck.

Before slinking into my bedroom, I used up all the hot water trying to scrub the human debris off. I spent a further ten minutes washing down the tub, cleaning my bloody footprints off the floor and disposing of my clothes. It was the least I could do.

I quickly closed the bedroom door behind me, the trill of my mobile phone hurrying my movements. 'Nikki,' I breathed, seeing that this was the fourth time she'd rung.

'Where are you?' she hissed, dispensing with pleasantries.

'I think I'm grounded.'

'What? Why?'

'It's complicated.'

'So, sneak out.'

Honestly, the thought appealed to me but was quickly shoved onto the backburner—when I snuck out, people tended to get dead. 'I can't.'

'Sure you can.'

'Nikki, I'm in quite a bit of trouble. I really don't want to upset my parents any more than I already have.'

'Connor's asking about you,' Nikki teased, lowering her voice enticingly. That wasn't going to work. There was no way I was going out that window again tonight.

I raked a hand through my wet hair, untangling the ends with my fingers. A nervous thrill coursed through me, but I wouldn't get my hopes up despite Nikki's encouragement. As far as I knew, Connor was still dating Heather Bitchface. 'Are you sure?'

'Ah-huh.'

'What about Heather? I thought they were bumping uglies?'

Nikki scoffed. 'My source tells me it was just a vay-kay romance.'

'Your source?' I screwed my face up. 'That doesn't make me feel any better.'

Nikki giggled. 'What? I'm sure Connor's showered since then.'

'Sick.'

'So are you coming, or what?'

'Or what.'

'No,' she groaned. 'You helped me organise this and so far it's been really fun. People are still showing up, so security won't lock you out if you turn up just yet.'

I dropped onto the edge of my bed, assessing the end of my locks with a distracted air. 'Nikki, are you sure that you want me to sneak out of my house, walk all the way through Zone Two alone, all the while praying I don't run into a flesh-eating zombie?' A small, twisted smile was upon my lips.

'Fucking zombies,' Nikki mumbled. 'They're ruining our social life.'

This time I did snicker, amused by her irritation and my deception. I only stopped when I could no longer hear her and the phone line echoed sounds of struggle and static. 'Nikki?'

More mumbled voices joined the chorus of noise, before I heard, 'Katie, is that you?'

My mouth went dry, my tongue suddenly like sandpaper. Hearing the sound of Connor's dulcet tones was both a surprise and a pleasure, unless of course he'd commandeered the phone to recommend me a great pimple cream? After all, he'd liked Heather's last Facebook status, a post that had pinpointed my recent flaws.

'Connor?'

'Why aren't you here?' he demanded.

'Grounded.'

'So sneak out.'

Wow. Did everyone at school constantly piss on their parent's rules? My parents were awesome—who else would have brought me home a hamster, those cats, a puppy and a few of the older neighbours? 'I can't. Besides, I really don't want to upset my parents any more than I already have. Sneaking around after dark in any Zone is just plain stupid.'

'Why are you in trouble?' Connor asked me.

'Um …' I frowned, yet another hypocritical admission about to spring forth from my lips. 'I snuck out of Zone Two.'

Connor started to laugh, the action bringing a reluctant smile to my lips. 'What a hypocrite,' he chuckled. 'Tell you what. I have a car, so I can come and pick you up, as long as you can sneak out of the house and meet me out front.'

'I'm not sure that my parents will buy into your logic once I'm busted a second time.'

'Come on, Katie.'

I shook my head, the goodie-two-shoes firmly fixed on my feet. 'Sorry, Connor, not tonight.'

'Fine.' A few seconds of silence passed between us. 'I guess I'll be coming to you then.'

'What the—' It was too late, he'd already hung up. I tried re-dialling Nikki but the call was going straight to voicemail.

Fuck.

I had several seconds of sheer and utter panic. My bed sheets smelt like the sweaty fat folds of a Weight Watcher's dropout, and here I was sitting around in Hello Kitty pyjamas.

Minutes passed. I sat perched on the end of my mattress, wondering if I should put on a bra, blow dry my hair or start modelling some Victoria Secret.

Fuck.

I shot up from the edge of the bed and threw open my wardrobe doors. I wrangled on a bra—nothing worse than saggy boobs—then slipped on some denim shorts, silently patting myself on the back for razoring earlier and committing to a deforestation of the leg variety. I modelled three extra-tight t-shirts before settling on a pink one, with the slogan *Can't Touch This* on the front and *Kidding* on the back.

I lathered myself with both deodorant and perfume, spritzing lavender oil in every direction before opening the window to air out the stale fart smell. Next, I ran to the mirror. I didn't have time to do a full make-up regime, so I squirted a globule of concealer onto my palms and rubbed it into my face like sunscreen. I was baffled by the length of time it was taking to make me beautiful.

My head snapped to the right as I heard a profanity muttered from just below my bedroom window. I raced to the ledge and stuck my head out. Connor was dangling below, one foot braced on the guttering, the other on the trellis-work conveniently running up alongside my window.

'Help me up,' Connor whispered, reaching a hand out to me. Poor fella. I really was starting to wonder how he came to be one of the best athletes in school.

Reaching down and clasping his hand in mine, I hauled him up the last few feet and onto the window ledge. His shoes were scrambling to find purchase on the outside walls, so I grabbed the back of his pants and yanked him the rest of the way inside. Connor fell into my room with a soft *thump*.

My eyes were immediately drawn to the back of my bedroom door, certain it would be flung open any second by an angry parent. Thankfully, there were no footfalls on the stairs beyond, no shouts of protest.

When I looked back at Connor he was still hauling himself to his feet and dusting off his jeans. He looked exhausted from the short climb. His continued, sharp pants suggested that he seriously needed to work on his cardio.

My smile faded as a darting shadow in the backyard below stole my attention. 'Did you bring anyone with you?' I asked, moving quickly to the ledge and studying the yard. Leaves bobbed gently in the breeze, the rear spotlight casting eager beams of light across the expanse of grass. Nothing appeared out of place.

Was I seeing things?

'Why would I bring someone?'

'I thought I saw something out there,' I murmured, scouting the yard. I stopped when another small movement caught my eye, a darkened corner near the fence line producing a larger shadow than usual. Could it be another zombie, or was it just a neighbourhood pet or stray animal?

'Holy shit,' Connor hissed, falling back to his knees and crawling over to the window. 'Did I just run through a zombie-infested backyard?'

I frowned at his crouching form huddled by my legs. 'I don't know if it's a zombie,' I answered honestly, 'but I *did* tell you not to come.'

Connor took a minute to study the yard for himself. Satisfied, he rose slowly to his feet, towering over me by at least a head—a very attractive one at that. 'I wanted to come.'

His hot breath on the side of my face and the drop in his tone distracted me long enough to glance away from the window. I instead found myself looking at the lushness of his mouth, my imagination once again concocting all manner of sexual scenarios between us.

Any worries of a zombie lurking in my backyard were soon forgotten the second I closed that gap and lifted my lips to his. They were softer than I'd imagined and sweet, an indulgence I wished to partake of on so many levels. I couldn't help including the hint of blood that filled the tiny capillaries within on that list.

I tasted him eagerly, miraculously keeping my eager teeth in check, exploring his mouth with my tongue. His low groans of pleasure spurred me on. Our hands were everywhere, Connor clearly ignoring the slogan on my shirt. He tasted of honey and goodness, and though a part of me was suppressing the instinct to bite him, the predator within was surprisingly disinterested.

'Katie,' he breathed against my parted lips, panting and at a loss for words.

'I'm sorry,' I mumbled, placing a palm against his chest to force a distance between us. 'I didn't mean to do that.'

'I'm glad you did.'

'Yeah, but you and Heather ...' I was testing the waters, making sure Nikki's supposed sources were to be relied upon.

'I'm not with Heather. We had a few dates over the vacation break but it was nothing serious.'

'Are you still attracted to her?'

A wry smile crossed his lips as he tugged me closer, wrapping his arms around my waist. 'Some parts of her.'

I groaned, Heather's rather impressive D-cups coming instantly to mind.

Connor cackled at my forlorn expression. Remembering I was not alone in the house, he quickly clapped a hand over his mouth and studied my bedroom door in silence. A few moments later, he removed his hand. 'I won't lie. Heather's attractive but she's also a nasty bitch. What I did like were her connections, namely her uncle's beach house and the security he could have provided for the Beach Bonanza this year.'

'You social whore,' I teased, feeling a tad better, though still unable to shake images of Connor and Heather together. 'If you were using Heather for her beach house, what are you hoping to get out of me?'

'Tips for winning the marathon?' he suggested, running his hands slowly up and down my back.

I scoffed, allowing the slow journey his hands were making down to my rear end. A gentle squeeze and a decisive pull, and we were suddenly pressed very intimately together. 'Here's a tip—forget about the marathon. You couldn't outrun a zombie, let alone beat me.'

Connor inched closer, lowering his head and moving past my eager lips until he nuzzled the soft flesh of my neck. 'Are you sure about that?'

My eyelids fluttered. My knees felt weak but I was determined to make my point, albeit breathily and half-drugged with lust. 'Connor, my grandma can run faster than you, and she uses a walking frame.'

His grumbled response was entirely lost as those probing lips once again sought solace against mine. Protesting was for those who didn't know what they wanted, and I knew that I wanted Connor. With insistent tongues and roaming hands, I handed myself over to his exploration, feeling certain I could kiss him forever.

A part of me was still confused. Why wasn't I overcome with rabid hunger?

As we collapsed backwards onto my bed, his body prone against mine and our lips delighting in the taste of one another, I wondered if we'd rushed this next step. Clothes started to come off and …

I mentally slapped myself. I'd forgotten to brush the homeless guy from out of my teeth.

CHAPTER FOUR

Dear Diary,

Connor and I are officially a thing, and Heather Rosenthal can kiss my hairy bum. We spent Saturday night making out, and props to me for not ~~chewing~~ kissing his face off or giving it up on the first date.

I let him touch my boobs and he practically opened his pants for return favours. I declined. I guess I'm just not that kind of girl.

Anyway, Nikki didn't get up me about missing the lock-in, especially since telling her about Connor spending the night in my bed. Mum, however, flipped her lid when she found his underwear on the floor the next day.

I've got to see Dr Chalmers again today. I've also got Home Economics first up, and I have to make a meringue. Both of these things make me want to poke my eyeballs out. I'll let you know how it goes.

Katie xo

I stood in front of the oven door, peering through the onyx-tinted glass at the dilapidated pile of whipped egg within. Clearly, I'd done something seriously wrong. For one, it looked like I was cooking a Frisbee; and, two, a smell like a sulphur pit was emanating from within.

'Hmm,' Mrs Cook sighed, as she bent down beside me. 'I

think you might have got some yolk in it. Did you use the egg separator?'

'I was supposed to separate the egg?'

I imagined if she wasn't so composed in her floral dress, ballet flats and carefully applied make-up, Mrs Cook might have slapped her forehead with incredulity. 'You're basically cooking a sweet omelette right now, Katie.'

'I guess that explains why it smells like shit.'

'Language.'

'Sorry.'

Mrs Cook sighed, standing back up. 'You might as well pull it out.' She glanced at the flashy gold watch strapped to her left wrist. 'There's no time to make another one. I won't be able to pass you on this.'

'But I got the main ingredient right.'

She waved an impatient hand at the oven. 'Clean your station up.'

'Yes, Mrs Cook.'

'And, Katie?'

'Yes?'

'Start reading through your Cooking Basics handbook. I don't want to have to fail you again this semester.'

I nodded, switching the oven off and quickly dragging my egg pie out of the heat. A few snickers erupted from the mouths of those closest, but I paid them no heed. I was betting no one else in the room could skin a cat in under a minute flat.

With another failed Home Economics class done for the morning, I sped from the room like it was on fire and headed for biology. Naturally, Heather did her best to make me feel welcome, mentioning how my bee-sting shaped boobs had apparently poked her in the eye as I'd passed.

I was about to retort with a stream of lesbian taunts, when

Connor piped up as he slipped through the door behind me, holding out his upturned palm and jesting that my boobs actually fit quite nicely. A round of wolf-whistles erupted from the meatheads in the football team behind us. That shut her up.

I'd honestly thought Heather was going to be another obstacle in the path to Connor's affections, and I couldn't help but feel a little deflated by how easily the battles I'd suspected Heather and I would have had this semester were avoided. I mean, all I'd really done was taken my shirt off.

Connor brought me back to the present by wrapping a protective arm around my shoulder. I couldn't help but stiffen, old habits dying hard. I was well-fed from the weekend, but I might already have had a head-scab brewing or some sort of oozy pus trying to make headway out of my ear canals. I hadn't given myself the once-over since school started, and I didn't want Connor to find any flaws.

'You free this afternoon?' he asked, nuzzling my neck. All must have been well; he didn't pull away, and he certainly didn't throw me down and try to blow my head off with one of the emergency, standard issue handguns kept within every classroom.

'I'd like to say "yes", but I can't. I have an appointment.'

'What about after?'

We settled onto one of the back lab benches together, his arm still around me, holding me near. I almost felt a little sorry for Heather as she glanced back at us, her eyes narrowed and lips pursed with discontent. 'Um, to be honest, I can't.'

Connor flashed me puppy dog eyes, so blue I found myself unable to look away. 'Aww, come on, Katie.'

'I don't know, Connor, my mum is still pretty pissed about finding your undies on my bedroom floor.'

'I promise to keep them on this time.'

I giggled. 'We'll see.'

'I'll just climb through your bedroom window again,' he pressed, his fingers drawing patterns on my upper arms.

'You mean you'll try, and then I'll have to haul your ass the rest of the way up?'

'Is your main aim to constantly emasculate me?'

'Oh God, no,' I said, quickly studying his face to ensure he was joking. 'You do that all on your own.'

Connor gasped in mock horror, slamming a fist against his heart as if my words had fatally wounded him. He collapsed onto the lab bench beside me, arms sprawled across the sparkling white surface. A few onlookers studied us with interest.

I rolled my eyes at his antics, catching Heather's intense gaze from across the room. The way her eyes surveyed every last inch of my body sent a small shiver skating up the length of my spine. I felt a little unnerved, confronted by the prospect of a slightly different breed of predator. Perhaps this victory wouldn't be so easy after all?

I was suddenly very excited by the possibility of a challenge, the same way I'd felt the other night while claiming the homeless man from the shadowy figure below the underpass. Was it possible for a mere cheerleader to elicit this type of response from within? Was it possible that that shadowy figure had been Heather Rosenthal, herself another member of the walking dead like me who was hiding amongst the normalcy of society? Were her parents hiding her from the authorities like mine were? Was Heather the one who killed Mr Chan?

No. There was no way Heather could be a zombie, unless something had happened to her over the vacation break.

While I'd been speculating, Connor had been talking

again. I'd heard nothing, my eyes still locked on those angry, green ones studying me from afar. I was seriously going to have to keep my eye on her, if for no other reason than the increasing scrutiny she was now showing me. I couldn't afford to be caught. I couldn't afford to let another zombie eat key members of my town and lead the authorities to my door.

I guess Heather Rosenthal was going down after all.

* * *

Dr Chalmers was wearing a bright red pantsuit today. Ordinarily, I wouldn't have paid much attention but the colour evoked all kinds of unexpected reactions from within. With matching lipstick, her pale skin and auburn hair stood out against her monochromatic colour scheme.

Her make-up was immaculate, carefully applied to cover any possible flaws that may have been lingering beneath those layers of foundation. Her dark eyes twinkled with vitality, her finger and toenails painted to match her flashy pantsuit.

'Are you all right, Katie?' she asked, concern dripping from her voice.

I shook my head, embarrassed that she'd noticed my physical inventory. 'Sorry. Yeah, I'm fine.'

'You seem distracted today.'

Was that a question or statement? 'I'm okay.'

Dr Chalmers crossed one slim leg over the other, rustling the synthetic material of her pants in the process. She reached for her pen and notepad, holding them ready as if I might actually divulge something interesting enough to note. 'How was school today?'

'Average.'

'Katie, you're in a safe place. Anything that you decide to discuss with me is completely confidential.'

'I know,' I murmured, steely as ever in my resolve.

'Tell me a little about your friends at school, about who you might like or dislike.'

'Why?'

She smiled politely, shifting only slightly. 'Sometimes it helps to have someone to talk to about the things you can't discuss with your friends or your parents.'

'I trust my parents.'

'Of course you do,' Dr Chalmers agreed, nodding sympathetically, 'but clearly your parents believe trust is not enough. They brought you to me because they think you need someone impartial to talk to, someone who can understand what you are going through.'

I began to laugh, though the amusement was fleeting. 'No offence, but you can't really help me at all.'

'Katie, you haven't even tried talking to me yet.'

'Because I *know* you can't help me.'

'Why don't you start by trying to tell me what's bothering you?'

'I can't.'

'You can't or you won't?' she probed, leaning forward slightly in her chair.

'Both.'

Dr Chalmers wrote something short and sweet among her notes and then refocused her large, dark eyes upon me once more. 'Why don't you tell me about Connor? You mentioned his name last time you were here.'

'You want to talk about the guy I've just started dating?'

'Let's focus specifically on your feelings and urges.'

My eyes narrowed exponentially. 'My mum's already had the sex talk with me, so we can skip over that.'

Dr Chalmers allowed herself a brief smile. 'I was more curious about how you think and feel about the situation.'

I shrugged. 'Well, I do like kissing him.'

She studied the notepad in front of her again, pen flying furiously over the page. 'And how do you feel during this activity?'

'Good, I guess.'

'And how far have things progressed between the two of you?'

I folded my arms across my chest, shifting uncomfortably in the wood-backed seat. 'Is it weird talking about this? It feels weird to me. Can we talk about something else?'

'It's perfectly normal to have urges, Katie.'

'I know that,' I said quickly, my eyes scanning the room, looking everywhere but back into the scrutiny in my therapist's eyes. 'I just don't want to talk about them.'

Dr Chalmers shifted in her seat, disappointment spreading across her features like the heat that had bathed mine with shame. 'All right then. You're a teenager, so why don't you tell me instead about someone who might be causing you to feel angry?'

Heather Rosenthal immediately came to mind. 'I can't think of anyone.'

'No teenager is of an even temperament all the time.'

'Well, of course, I get pissed off every now and then but—'

'Look, Katie,' she interrupted. 'I can't help you if you don't help me.'

I held my hands up in surrender, confused. 'I don't know what it is that you want me to tell you.'

'Just be honest with me.'

'I don't—'

'Trust me?'

'Um, yeah.'

'Hmm.' Dr Chalmers furiously penned additional notes, her white-knuckled grip flying across the pages of her notepad as she chewed the corner of her lower lip. Miraculously, her red lipstick remained completely intact and her white teeth stayed absent of the stain. 'I heard the school had a lock-in on Saturday night. Did you go?'

'I was grounded.'

'Interesting,' she remarked. 'And, why is that?'

Careful, Katie. 'The usual. Doing stuff I shouldn't have.'

'Such as?'

'Isn't time up yet?' I asked, searching the bleak office for a clock.

There was a long pause. Dr Chalmers had stopped scribbling notes and was eyeing me critically. She'd uncrossed her legs and was sitting on the edge of her seat, fingers clasping her kneecaps. 'Katie, if there's anything you ever need, anything that you think you might not be able to tell me about, please know that you can. I will listen to whatever it is without prejudice.'

Her words resonated deeply, full of an underlying meaning that set my teeth on edge and left a pit of unease in my stomach. Did Dr Chalmers know my secret?

I figured it best to trust only in myself, so I just said, 'Thank you, Dr Chalmers. I really do appreciate the offer, and I promise I'll take you up on it if something major comes along.'

Dr Chalmers blinked, her scarlet lips parting slightly as she digested my answer. 'At least promise me you'll keep up the writing in your diary. You are doing that, aren't you?'

'I am.'

'Are you finding it therapeutic?'

'I guess.'

'It forces you to expose yourself, doesn't it?'

That was an interesting choice of words. 'I don't know. Who's really interested in the ramblings of a teenage girl, anyway?'

A pregnant pause followed before she replied, an answer that did little to ease my apprehension. 'I am.'

CHAPTER FIVE

Dear Diary,

There's been another death in Zone Three. It's the third zombie-related attack in the last few weeks. They found the homeless guy ~~conveniently slaughtered~~ *beneath the underpass and now it looks as if one of the security guards patrolling the Zone crossing has also been murdered.*

Clearly, ~~there's competition~~ *we have a problem.*

The Beach Bonanza has been cancelled, so Connor's pissed, mostly because he believed getting down and dirty in the sand was an option. It really wasn't.

Nikki's still pushing for the winter formal to go ahead. The school keeps taking her protests under advisement, but are insisting it only be held on the school grounds and that extra security be paid for by the formal committee. Nikki's okay with that; the rest of us aren't.

Heather's been watching me like a hawk and making my life a misery. On top of all the nasty-ass comments she's being whispering about me within earshot, the bitch keeps spreading rumours that I have chlamydia. So far Connor hasn't taken the bait, but Nikki thinks that's because he's seventeen and wants to get laid regardless. I'm more concerned about what diseases I could give Connor. Swapping spit seems harmless enough but tangling with my nether region?

Virgin suicide.

Katie xo

I studied the track in front of me—endlessly winding, it was edged by an unsightly length of long, feathery grass that whispered in the early morning breeze, a soft accompaniment to my pounding footfalls and the even breaths that puffed out from between my parched lips.

Small rises and falls marked the overgrown path, a sure sign that no one had used the track in over a year. A layer of dust covered the once-compact ground, springing up around my ankles in a dirty plume that marked my socks and sweat-slicked knees.

The sporadic chirping of early rising birds in the bushes beyond could be heard, but the area around the path was otherwise quiet. I'd come alone, wanting to take my time while rediscovering this old marathon track that had been closed to the general public due to the recent zombie attacks.

I had no idea who the 'general public' actually referred to, but I was assuming it referred to humankind and so didn't apply to me.

I was bummed out that the marathon had been cancelled. I'd been training for over a year, often taking the time before school—but mostly after—to get my body in shape for the big event. Public safety was a priority, but the situation was still annoying.

I pumped my legs harder, imagining that I was running the forty kilometre stretch against competition. I relished the feel of the cool breeze that tickled my cheeks, of the air that rushed through my nose and burning lungs as I drove my legs harder and faster.

I wasn't often alone these days. Between my eagle-eyed parents, Nikki trying to involve me in every school-based activity going, and Connor's blatant and ongoing affections, it was small wonder I had time to feed, let alone run.

Speaking of feeding ... that homeless guy had kept me

fresh for well over a week, but the lingering effects of the rabbit Mum had brought home a few days ago were starting to wear off. Exercise would be a risk—my scent currently ranged from a stale, unwashed pong to just plain nasty.

I really needed to hunt for fresh meat while I was out on the trail, or I'd just be asking for a haranguing by the locals.

My pace slowed. Strangely enough, I began to smell a hint of sweet perfume in the air—vanilla mixed with jasmine. I supposed it could have been from soap, as I'd certainly lathered enough of the stuff over myself to overcome my own zombie odour. Perhaps whoever or whatever was out there was doing the same.

I approached a sharp bend in the path and the smell grew stronger. I got the feeling that when I rounded that curve, whatever had braved the outdoors would be there, lurking or passing by. Either prospect was a little unsettling considering that the track was currently supposed to be closed.

A whisper of grass grazed my lower calves as I moved, determined not to completely break my stride lest I needed to start running a hell of a lot faster. My arms pumped at my sides, my senses on high alert.

That curve in the track came and went without incident, and I began to scan the trees and the path behind me with critical eyes. The scent of vanilla had turned cloying, growing to a pervasive sweetness that had become the very oxygen I breathed.

Yet, there was no one in sight. I knew I couldn't possibly be alone, but did I dare follow the smell and stray from the path to investigate further?

Shit. I really couldn't help myself.

Dust swirled around my ankles as I veered off to the left and into a tall thicket of grass. Feathery seed pods grabbed like tiny fingers at my shirt and pulled insistently at the fabric. They seemed to be begging me to go back.

I wandered deeper into the trees, the shadows growing long despite the rising sun at my back. My heart thudded heavily in my chest, uncertainty and fear unfurling and spreading to my limbs. An unquenchable dryness scratched at my throat.

A glimpse of something green—greener than the foliage of the closest trees and their multihued leaves—disappeared into a small clearing. Then there was another flash of lime-green brilliance. It stirred my growing unease.

I ducked behind a particularly large trunk, taking the time to calm myself. Clearly someone was out here with me. Whether they were friend or foe was a mystery, although I had my suspicions.

I scanned the trees once more, eyes straining for another glimpse of that unnatural material amongst the flora. I couldn't see anything out of the ordinary.

Then the sudden, almost shocking, scent of fresh meat stole away my attention completely.

My palms hit the dry earth and brush, my nose now tilted to the wind as I inhaled as deeply as I could. The sweet scent of that manufactured perfume was now fading, to be replaced by that of gore and fresh-spilt blood.

I crawled forward, ducking out from behind the tree trunk and out into the open. I was struck with a predator's dilemma—should I follow the perfume or follow the scent of the hunt?

A strangled gasping made the decision for me, leading me onwards to a small copse of trees a few yards away. The hunt was on—my prey was clearly wounded, if not already dying. There was no wild animal in the world that could cry out quite like a human could.

'Help me.'

I crawled forward, my hands and knees now chaffed from the raw earth and dry brush beneath me. There was a pain in the air that was palpable. The sounds of gurgling blood emanating from that throat appealed directly to my lingering humanity, and the inner me cringed. I could imagine feet scrabbling for purchase under the assault, a horror I was all too familiar with.

'Please … don't kill me.'

I surveyed the trees a final time. The woman was so close now that I could practically taste her fear. I began to salivate as my instincts took over; I felt the urgent need to lick her bones clean and suck out their marrow, despite being disgusted by such thoughts.

For the hundredth time, I thought, 'Thanks, Popmade. Thanks.'

Then the predator within took over.

I brushed aside a clump of foliage, drawing a frightened gasp from what I'd thought was a stranger. To attack had been the game plan, but the strangled scream that bubbled up in her throat and the fear in those impossibly wide, brown eyes stilled my actions. Staring back at me like a deer caught in the headlights, her bloodied lips parted and my name on the tip of her tongue, was Mrs Cook.

I froze, uncertain what to do. About ninety per cent of my being wanted to snap her neck and eat out her entrails. The other ten per cent was thinking more clearly. This situation was eerily similar to my recent encounter under the underpass. I was being set up, followed or even challenged—but by whom?

The fading scent of jasmine and vanilla still lingered in the air.

'K-katie,' she gasped, reaching shaking fingers out to me.

Her digits hung between us like a bridge over a ravine. I could take hold, pull her to me and take my fill, but eating her just because she was failing me at cookery seemed harsh. Plus, the coincidence was still too great.

I closed the distance between us and clasped her shaking hands in mine. 'Mrs Cook,' I sobbed, adding a few tears to reflect the suitable level of emotion. 'What happened to you?'

I did a physical inventory. There was bruising around her neck that seemed to suggest attempted strangulation, which on its own was strange. If this was a zombie attack the offender wouldn't have bothered with suffocation; they'd have dug right in, perhaps snapping the neck beforehand as I often did when trying to be humane.

Her left arm was dislocated, and by the looks of the bloody and exposed sinew of her legs, she had been dragged across rugged terrain. Her flesh had peeled away as it'd rubbed against the rocky debris and prickly grass. Sadly, she'd also been slashed right across the centre of her stomach. Hers would be a slow and painful death.

Poor Mrs Cook. There was nothing I could really do to ease her pain and I doubted even swift medical attention would save her. The wound across her stomach was too ragged and looked chewed, which meant that Mrs Cook would either die soon or risk succumbing to the disease that ravaged my teenage body.

I was betting that she'd die first. It only took hours to turn, but she clearly didn't have that, and if by some miracle she was rescued, without a cure she'd either be shot by the armed forces or sent to the desert.

'It was a zombie,' Mrs Cook finally managed to splutter. 'I think I'm going to die.'

I looked away, finding it difficult to ignore the vast amounts of blood that stained the dusty earth, blood that covered her frilly, yellow-striped skirt. I could see torn muscle glistening between the folds of her ravaged flesh and that made me want to jump her, rip open her guts and find out what other delectable prizes waited inside.

To distract myself, I thought through my options. Eating Mrs Cook was no longer on the table. Putting her out of her misery was also not feasible, as humane as that sounded. I couldn't pick her up and carry her back to civilisation. The authorities would wonder how a skinny girl like me, alone and without help, could carry her Home Economics teacher over twenty kilometres back to civilisation. I'd also have to explain why I was out running on a closed marathon track, which was a definite infringement of at least two Zone regulations.

Yet, I had to do something. I couldn't just let my teacher die in the middle of the scrub, alone and possibly riddled with the flesh-eating virus that had plagued the last year of my life. How could I help Mrs Cook without condemning myself?

'Mrs Cook, I don't know what to do,' I whispered. I was truly stumped.

Katie Palmer, speechless and without action? Nikki would have a fit.

'G-get out of h-here!' she rasped, squeezing my fingers with more strength than I would have thought possible. 'It's n-not safe.'

'Tell me how to help you.'

Because I just want to eat your face. I forced my brain to concentrate on something else entirely. Sudoku. Yes, Sudoku was a fabulous game, sometimes difficult and a great way to—

'Katie. Please, l-leave me here. I'm dead, anyway.'

I cringed. What she said made sense. No one would ever

know or suspect that I'd been there. Yes, there were fresh running trails on the track but a zombie could have easily made those. The undead still wore Nike joggers—all the better for them to catch you with, or so they say.

'If I leave you,' I started, my voice surprisingly fraught with emotion, 'the zombie may come back and finish what they started.'

'She w-won't,' Mrs Cook slurred, her eyes now drooping, her face impossibly white and slick with cold sweat.

'So it was a *she*?' I pressed, squeezing her fingers to keep her alert.

'Run, Katie.'

'Yes, yes,' I urged, frustrated that her voice was fading almost as quickly as the light behind her eyes. 'I will run, I promise, but first tell me: Do you know who the zombie is?'

Mrs Cook's lips moved but there was only silence.

'No,' I barked, giving her a gentle slap on the face, followed by a slightly harder one when she failed to respond. 'Tell me, Mrs Cook, who is the zombie?'

'She's coming for you.'

She's coming for me?

Those were the last words to slip past Mrs Cook's bloodied lips before the breath left her body a final time. My former teacher's eyes turned glassy and lifeless, staring straight up at me as if they still held something she wanted to convey.

I placed her hand gently down on her chest, releasing her fingers one by one. Mrs Cook looked almost peaceful now, except for those still-staring eyes. I considered closing the lids, but wondered if that might make it obvious that someone had been here when she'd passed.

I didn't want to leave her body to be picked at by other zombies, discarded in the brush like some piece of rubbish, but I really had little choice.

I rose slowly to my feet, brushing debris from my palms and knees, checking for stray splashes of blood or gore about my person. My hands were the only part of me carrying the evidence of Mrs Cook's demise, and if I did have a stalker, I certainly didn't want them to see me sticking those blood-slicked fingers in my mouth.

Scanning the tree line once more, I found little evidence that a threat still lingered. The scent of perfume had long since departed, but caution was a card I had to play, especially in light of the homeless man debacle. My hurried, amateur approach then could have resulted in the seeming vendetta being waged against me now.

Turning on my heel, I started to run, infinitely faster than I had before. I rounded corners like I was on rails, jumped over ditches and gradually increased my stride. My footfalls slapped along the ground with purpose, the tall grass scratching at my legs as I powered into the distance.

I headed towards home, and this time I would seek counsel from those older and wiser than myself—my parents.

The trees flew past in a blur, sweat pouring from my orifices with more haste than I would have liked. I could smell myself and was not a fan.

I hadn't had the opportunity to hunt, and as I continued to exert more and more energy, I could feel my hunger stirring. I wouldn't yet be a danger to those around me, but it wouldn't be long before my outside started to closely resemble my insides.

These troubling thoughts remained with me as I burst through a canopy of trees and re-entered the abandoned car park I'd left behind a few hours before, as I was starting my sojourn into the wild.

As I came to a stop, my feet skidding across the dusty

terrain, that perfume from before rose up and was on me once more, saturating the air with its sweetness.

I tried to remain calm, sucking in a deep lungful of breath, shaking out my legs and rolling my shoulders. I searched the quiet expanse, irritated by the niggling sensation of tightness in my calves, but not nearly as annoyed as I was by the morning's events. I'd really been dropped in the thick of it. *She's coming for you.* The words echoed through my head, both a threat and a warning. I'd already survived the worst of the zombie apocalypse, the brains being blown out on the pavement, the bodies, the horror. Yes, I was currently infected, but I was a high-functioning zombie. I may have had to spill blood for survival, but I was also hanging on for a cure, just like everyone else.

A parked car sat idle a few hundred meters down the road. With rusting headlights and chipped, pale blue paint covering the bonnet, the vehicle resembled all the other shitheaps still being driven since the original break out.

Survivors knew that off-road vehicles with bull bars and extra-large gas tanks were the only credible option these days. Mercedes and expensive Beamers were only good for ploughing into uncontrollable flesh-eaters. Matchbox-sized Asian vehicles were laughable, with their plastic materials and cheap locking mechanisms. Drivers didn't bother with ownership or registration papers now since half the population was dead, so identifying someone from their vehicle alone was virtually impossible.

What was a car doing out near a closed marathon track at this time of the morning, anyway? I didn't remember seeing it when I'd arrived or had I simply not noticed?

Another clue?

There was the slightest of movements inside the cabin. I'd originally assumed that the bulky shape might have been a butchered headrest, but could now see the outline of the driver—pardon the pun—sitting as still as the dead.

I faced the vehicle, fingers twitching at my sides as a sense of unease rose within me. This voyeur was either my zombie stalker or a random bystander, witness to the fact I'd recently been within the vicinity of a murder. I had no choice but to neutralise this threat.

I squared my shoulders and lifted my chin, the muscles in my legs bunching in preparation for flight. As my heels left the ground, my movements were tracked by the silhouette. The engine kicked over with relative ease. A flash of head-lights blinded all vision, dashing my hopes of identifying the driver.

My legs pumped faster and faster as they attempted to flee.

Executing a hurried U-turn, the car kicked forward. Loose gravel spewed from the rear tyres, the car fishtailing on the softer dirt before tearing a set of new tracks onto the adjoining highway.

Try as I might to catch up, I was soon nothing but a sweaty speck with greasy black hair in my voyeur's rear view mirror. I may have been a zombie and much faster than average, but I didn't have a V8 engine under the hood.

I broke off my pursuit, taking note of the make and model of the car, including the licence plate. 'Fuck!' I screamed, as the tail-lights faded into the early morning mist, nature itself seemingly against me as it swallowed up my adversary whole.

I was in serious trouble. I had only one option now—tell the authorities the truth about my training schedule and about my brief sojourn into the Zone in defiance of their regulations.

I was such an idiot.

Still cursing, I turned in the opposite direction and

headed for home. I was clearly out of my league. My parents were the only ones who could help me now without prejudice. At least, I hoped they'd help. Mum was still pretty pissed off about finding Connor's undies on my bedroom floor.

I really *had* been asking for trouble lately.

* * *

Running home proved a challenge all of its own. People were already stirring within their homes and throwing back their curtains to receive the early morning light, making it difficult for me to hide. Porch lights had been switched off, but ducking and weaving in the lingering shadows slowed my progress considerably. Thank God, I'd already eaten most of the neighbourhood's guard dogs.

Not far now. I dove over a small fence, finishing off with a commando roll across our front lawn that took me up to the threshold. I pounded on our front door, knowing it was deadlocked but would be opened after the usual checks were carried out.

'Mum, Dad,' I shouted through the mailbox slot, 'quick, open the front door!' A small part of me wondered if the desperation in my voice might make them reconsider, putting their own safety above and beyond that of the zombie teenager huddled on the stoop.

Almost immediately I could hear the pounding of footfalls on the stairs, followed by a cursory check of the front yard through the mailbox slot. When my mother's eyes fell upon my huddled form, the bronzed flap fell close and the dead bolt was released.

I quickly crawled inside as the door opened, Mum slamming it home behind me and re-securing all the locks.

'Oh, God,' Mum groaned, snapping a hand across her mouth and nose. 'You smell terrible, Katie.'

'Worse, I imagine.' I scrambled to my feet.

Dad bounded into the hallway and then seemed to immediately regret it as the smell hit him. He, too, placed his hand over his mouth and nose, eyes wide with panic. 'Katie? What's wrong? Where have you been?'

'I think I'm in trouble.'

Worried looks passed between them, fresh lines of concern already etching themselves upon Mum and Dad's faces. I felt terrible. The household was already tense, with them both attempting to hide recent arguments and hushed conversations behind closed doors.

Dad hated his new job even though Zone kickbacks meant more food rations for the family; Mum was bitter that she'd been relegated to the role of housewife since event co-ordinators—her former job—were now redundant; and, they both worried incessantly about Jack's well-being and morbid fascination with his slingshot. He'd recently moved on from harmless target practice to hunting anything that moved. Mrs Fraser had complained twice about Jack's lack of remorse after wounding her pug. I called it 'surviving'.

Perhaps Mum and Dad thought of our circumstances as an inescapable, soul-sucking burden?

'What is it, darling?' Mum asked, her voice nasal due to the fingers that were pinching her nostrils together.

'I know I've said this often lately, but please don't be mad.'

'Katie ...'

I rushed into my explanation, certain my words wouldn't make the least bit of difference. 'I got up early this morning to train, but I didn't take the car to the school grounds. Instead, I wanted to run at the old marathon track. Which, as you know, has been closed.' Their previous expressions of panic quickly changed, hurrying me to my point. 'Anyway, long story short, I found Mrs Cook and—'

'You ate her?' Dad finished, an even mixture of disgust and horror knotting his rigid shoulders.

'Hell, no!' I said. 'But she was attacked by another zombie. I tried to help her but Mrs Cook was already dying. There was so much blood.'

Neither parent made a move to comfort me, but that was no surprise. My hands were covered in blood, and I smelt like the rubbish dump. I fully expected them to usher me into the backyard, tip a bucket of bleach over my head, and sanitise me with a fire hose.

'Where is Mrs Cook now?'

'I had to leave her there. I was being followed.'

'Followed?' Dad asked, still annoyed.

'I haven't told you because I knew you'd freak out, but I think whoever did this to Mrs Cook has been following me since the day I killed that homeless guy, maybe even before. I can't be sure.'

Dad started to pace back and forth. He crossed his arms over his chest and then thinking better of it, re-plugged his nose. 'And you're only telling us this now? Katie, do you even realise how selfish that is? We have Jack's safety to consider, not to mention ourselves.' He kicked the base of the stair bannister, muttering under his breath, 'Now I'm late for my mindless, Zone-sanctioned job and I still have to sort this crap out.'

'I know, Dad. I'm so sorry. I didn't think much of it until Mrs Cook said that she was after me.'

'She?'

'Apparently.'

Dad was thoughtful for a moment. 'Were there any witnesses as you ran back here?'

'No, but—'

'Then this isn't so bad. No one saw you so—'

'That's the thing, Dad. When I came off the track there was someone watching me from a car. I couldn't be sure if it was the zombie or just a curious passerby. Either way, I tried to run after them but they got away.'

Dad started swearing like a trooper.

'Did you recognise the car?' Mum asked, frowning at the bad language coming from the other 'respectable' head of house.

'No, but I did get the licence plate.'

Mum and Dad were silent for several minutes, before finally Dad piped up.

'We have to tell the authorities,' he said, his voice tired. He ran nervous fingers through his hair and then straightened the tie he'd only had the chance to half-do up around his neck. He repeated the movement again and again.

'We can't do that,' Mum argued. 'Katie shouldn't have been on the marathon track to begin with. She was straddling the Zones at the time and was out before curfew at an unsanctioned, unmanned location.'

'But there could be a possible witness reporting her as we speak. We have to assume that's the course of action they will take and get in first. Katie, did you eat any part of Mrs Cook?' He was practically choking on those last words.

'Of course not, Dad. I know her. She was my teacher and she was trying to help me. Mrs Cook thought I was in danger.'

Dad moved to the hall table and picked up the receiver. 'Go upstairs and get cleaned up. You smell like the dead and look too guilty with your hands covered in all that blood. I'll call Zone Security and try to come up with a suitable excuse. You'll probably be heavily reprimanded for breaking Zone regulations but that can't be avoided at this point.'

'What if they want to test her?' Mum sobbed, her fingers still firmly pressed against her nose. 'There's no way we can keep her change a secret if they draw her blood.'

'It's a risk we'll have to take.'

I felt my bottom lip quivering, the seriousness of the situation pressing down on me. I was almost hyperventilating. The fear of being put down like cattle, or slapped with a collar and sent to a zombie pen at the ass end of the world, was making my stomach lurch. I'd really fucked up this time.

'Katie,' Dad shouted, snapping his fingers at me, 'go! And act suitably distressed about all this. If we're going to be investigated this morning, I need you to look like this whole experience has seriously shaken you up.'

'I won't need to act.'

'Good.' He looked directly at Mum, taking firm control of the situation at hand. 'Get her some meat, anything. I don't care if it's a rat. We can't afford for her to smell like that when they arrive.'

'Seriously, Dad. Rats?'

'Do you want your head blown off?' he snapped, covering the mouth piece of the phone.

Point taken.

* * *

I pressed my face against the living room doors, straining to listen to the stern conversation being held in the kitchen. Mum and Dad were mumbling, hopefully relaying my story to the authorities in the best light possible. I wasn't quite sure how you could smooth over a violation of Zone rules, but I suspected that my parents were giving it a damn good go. With this being the third murder in only a few weeks, Zone Security were itching to find someone to blame.

I sniffed my armpits—the second time in as many minutes. It risked becoming a nervous habit, or worse still, an obvious giveaway of my zombified state.

Mum had finally found some food. It wasn't rat—okay, I take that back—it was a rat with wings, a bloody pigeon that Jack had knocked out of the air with his slingshot from his bedroom window. Apparently, practice was permitted only when Mum and Dad were more worried about my exposure than encouraging Jack's possible sadistic streak.

Poor Jack. Their double standards must've been so confusing.

Anyway, pigeon sucks ass. I was still spitting lice and finding feathery fluff in my hair. I'd brushed and washed my face twice since, but the disease-ridden little bastard was still repeating on me, much like bad chilli from the school cafeteria.

I sniffed my armpits for the umpteenth time, finally satisfied that all was well. I'd double-scrubbed and lathered, slapped on body lotion and traced the wet areas with talcum powder. Adding a healthy dose of aroma therapy oils into the mix, I now smelt like retirement home crossed with high-class flower shop.

'She understands that she was violating Zone rules,' I heard my father say, now much clearer than before. He must have been shouting, or at the very least, annoyed enough to raise his voice.

'The risks involved are stupendous. For her to have even considered leaving the house without a companion and then proceed while knowingly breaking the law supersedes all logic. I have to wonder where such bravado comes from.' The new voice was husky, an octave past deep. The man sounded like he'd been chain-smoking his entire life.

'She's a teenager,' my mother reminded the security officers.

'Yes, exactly,' Mr Chain-smoker said. 'My point is exactly that. No teenager, despite their defiant nature, would wander willingly through the streets in the early hours of the morning unless they had nothing to fear.'

'There is always plenty to fear, especially with these most recent unprovoked attacks,' another voice added.

Someone snorted—I assumed it was my mother given the small, nerve-riddled burst of laughter that followed. 'Unprovoked? Since when do any of us need to provoke them? They attack because they're hungry.'

'Yes, but as Zone Security is tightening, they're making it harder and harder for the fresher ones to hunt without being caught. Case in point: your daughter finding that woman on the track today.'

'Do you think Katie interrupted them or perhaps scared the zombie away?'

There was a brief silence followed by the scraping of stools against the chipped linoleum floor. At first, I thought I'd missed something and that everyone was getting up to leave. In a moment of sheer panic, I crab-walked back towards the couch, threw myself over the arm and then pretended I was reading a magazine.

When minutes passed without interruption, I quickly scrambled up from the couch again and rushed back to the door, pressing my ear against the aged timber.

'Look, I'm just suggesting—'

'I know what you're suggesting,' my mother barked. 'Don't you think we've chastised her about this? She's been training for this marathon for over a year, training with friends most mornings. I suspect that Katie didn't think, she just did it!'

'But regardless, ma'am,' the slicker voice of the two began, 'she openly put herself in danger. You have to understand that we are suspicious as to why.'

'Of course, but—'

I rushed into the kitchen without thought, determined to defend my actions and support my parents. 'You don't understand how long I've been training for this marathon!' I gushed, my hands curling into angry fists at my sides. 'Before the apocalypse, I was set for scholarships to all the best schools. Eventually, I'd probably qualify for the Olympics.'

My parents hung their heads, clearly crestfallen that I'd made an appearance at all. The security officers, both bulky and covered in combat greens, jumped up from their chairs. I noted that Mr Chain-smoker had his hand on the gun in his holster, a practised gesture. Slick was a little more subtle but his fingers were twitching by his sides.

My parents specifically asked me to remain in the living room. If what just happened didn't highlight that I had a disobedient nature, nothing would.

'Please,' I moaned, trying hard to bring on the waterworks. 'I just wanted to do it. I wanted to run the track and beat my personal best. Yes, I knew that what I was doing was something stupid and I was sweating bullets the entire time, but I guess a part of me thought I could outrun them if they came after me.'

'Little girl,' Mr Chain-smoker interrupted, his fingers still brushing the butt of his gun, 'you are by far the most irresponsible and stupid person I have met in the Zones yet. No one goes outside Zone Security unless they have a death wish. Or, nothing to fear.'

I did not like that implication. 'Like it's safe in the Zones,' I shouted at him, tears of frustration now marking my cheeks. 'Three people, including one of your own, have been mauled and eaten in the last couple of weeks. Now my teacher has died and I had to witness it! It doesn't matter where I am or where I've been—you aren't doing your job properly!'

'Katie!' my mother warned, tugging on my elbow.

I shook her off, squaring my chin at the officers. 'What are you even doing to catch her killer? I held Mrs Cook's hand in mine while she gasped for breath, shitting myself and thinking that zombie would soon be coming back for me. And you sit here, at our kitchen table, accusing me instead of being, what, out there looking for them?'

'Little girl—'

'Don't you *little girl* me. I saw someone I know and care about die in front of me this morning. What exactly are you doing about that?'

The portly officer I'd referred to as Slick moved his hands to the table, folding them calmly in front of him. His counterpart still sat rigidly in his chair, hand on his gun and face set in a scowl so deep you could get lost in the folds of his forehead.

Slick sat forward, eyeing me speculatively. 'Katie, is it?'

'Yes,' I snapped, my hands automatically wiping the tears from my cheeks before settling defiantly on my hips.

'Katie, I can see you're upset and I can't imagine what you've been through this morning. It is a terrible trauma, but we do have to investigate all avenues. That's why we are here now.'

'But, I don't understand. Mum and Dad told you everything, told you about the car and the licence plate. Shouldn't you be chasing that lead?'

Slick offered me a polite smile. 'You see, Katie, this is

where the situation can get a little tricky. That car that you said you saw out on the road was registered to one of the Zone Two residents. Now, these residents all have alibis for this morning. Their neighbours back up the claim and swear that the car never moved from their driveway.'

'Who owns the car? What are their names?' Dad asked.

'We can't give you that information, sir. It would be in violation of the privacy act.'

'But whoever they are, they were definitely there!'

'Perhaps, but that's your word against theirs. Katie, in all honesty, they have a watertight alibi, so we won't be investigating that angle any further.'

'So you're saying that you're investigating me now?'

Mr Chain-smoker twitched in his seat, his face still set in grim lines. A silent look passed between him and Slick; Mum and Dad looked equally overcome with concern. Mum ran her hand up and down my back in soothing circles, but it didn't help. Not even the truth could help me now.

'Katie,' Slick continued, his voice calm and even, 'we have to be honest with you. We are investigating your violation of the regulations and nothing more.'

'What about Mrs Cook?'

'Truthfully, we haven't recovered any remains at this stage. We only have your story to go by.'

'What!' I screeched. 'Are you telling me Mrs Cook isn't out in the scrub?'

'At this stage, she is in fact missing. Locating her has proven to be an issue. We currently have security canvassing the area in the hopes that we may still find her.'

'Is it possible that the zombie came back for her?' my mother asked, doing her best to calm me down with her soothing touch.

Slick opened his palms on the table. 'Your guess is as

good as ours. Your phone call this morning was our first indication that Mrs Cook had possibly met with foul play, but since we haven't recovered a body we can only count her as missing at this stage. And Katie, I'm sorry to say that despite your best intentions to inform us, you've put yourself in the thick of it.'

'What does that even mean?' Dad asked, leaning forward across the table.

'It means, sir,' Mr Chain-smoker gruffly replied, 'that your daughter is under suspicion of being either a troublemaker or a member of the undead.'

Mum gasped, clasping a hand over her mouth. 'You think my baby girl could be one of those flesh-eaters?' She shook her head, grasping my hand tightly in hers. 'No. No, she can't be. Katie's always been a little defiant, but she's never … eaten anyone.'

Way to go Mum. She was laying it on thick—tears, a horror-filled gasp, and enough endearments to make me sound genuinely sweet and innocent. If I'd owned an Academy Award, I would have handed it to her.

Slick looked sympathetic, eyeing me from head-to-toe, wringing his fingers together. 'I'm so sorry, ma'am,' he said, directly addressing my mother. 'If it's any consolation, I do think Katie is just a little misguided and probably unaffected by disease. Unfortunately, we do have to be thorough for the sake of all the other residents of this Zone. Due to Katie's violation, she will be tested and your home will be searched. I can't apologise enough for the inconvenience, but we must do our jobs and ensure the safety of everyone concerned.'

Dad pushed back his chair, circling Mum and I with purpose before placing steadying hands on our backs. It was his way of telling us to stay silent and let him handle the situation from here. 'We understand, officers. When will this search and testing begin?'

'A team will be over within the hour. We expect full co-operation.'

'Of course,' Dad conceded. 'We want you to be thorough.'

I was fucked—there were no other words to describe how fucked I was. My worst fears had come to pass. I was a zombie and soon everyone would know it. Was it too late to bend over and kiss my ass goodbye?

CHAPTER SIX

Dear Diary,

It's likely that this will be my last entry. Zone Security suspects me of illicit activity—namely, of ingesting the living.

I can't tell you how pissed off I am right now. If Dad hadn't called Zone Security I'd ~~be in the clear~~ not be in this trouble. As it turns out, no one had called in an official sighting, so clearly ~~that fricken' zombie~~ someone is playing a vicious game with me.

Mum and Dad are frantically running around the house right now ~~to hide any possible evidence~~. Dad's going through the mulching pile in the backyard with a fine-toothed comb, and Mum's wiping every surface down with undiluted bleach. If that's not a dead giveaway that we've got something to hide, then I don't know what is. Well, except for the ~~pigeon in the neighbour's trash~~ fear of being unjustly accused.

I haven't called Nikki or Connor to tell them what's going on. How would I even explain it? Nikki and I are besties but would that mean anything if she thought I was a zombie?

Shit. What the hell am I going to do if I'm convicted?

Die, probably.

Katie xo

The house had been wiped clean. Mum and Dad were both sweating. Jack and I were sitting in the living room, nervous and unsure of what we should do or say to ease their obvious fears. Jack was holding my hand. It was the first time he'd touched me since he'd found out I could swallow him whole.

'What's gonna happen to you?' he whispered, squeezing his little fingers around my own.

'I don't know, Jack, but it'll be nothing good.'

'What if I show them my slingshot and how good I am at finding you food? Do you think they'll let you stay if they know you won't eat anyone?'

'I doubt it.'

Jack shifted on the couch, resting his head on the side of my arm. 'I don't want you to go.'

'Really? I thought I scared you sometimes.'

'Only when you smell real bad and your face starts to peel off. That's when I know that you might eat me ... but you never do.'

'Aww, Jack. I won't eat you.' *I think.* 'And I don't want to go either. But if the worst happens, I need you to be really brave for Mum and Dad. Especially Mum, because she's spinning out.'

'She washed the bathtub twice.' Jack snuggled closer, wrapping his spare arm around my midsection. 'Then she put those funny goggles on and shined that blue light all around your bedroom.'

Right. So she was checking for blood. Geez, what did Mum think she was, a part of the CSI team?

'Katie!'

Jack and I both jumped, surprised by the horrified outburst coming from upstairs. It continued, with my name being repeated again and again like a crazy mantra. Mum's voice held a seriously agitated edge.

Jack and I shared a *what's her problem?* look and snickered, sharing one last moment of sibling affection before I sighed and quickly unfolded him from around me. I left Jack on the couch, watching after me like I was going on a death-march. Considering the way Mum was screaming my name from the landing, perhaps I was.

I bounded up the stairs two at a time and found Mum frantically pacing between the hallway landing and my room. 'What's wrong?' I asked, following behind her.

When Mum ran into me on the return trip, she scoffed, shoved me to the side and began pacing in circles again. She continued, pacing backwards and forward, obviously wanting to make a decent attempt at wearing a trail in the carpet. Her arms were held tightly across her ample chest, her face a mass of seething anger.

'Mum, come on. Stop pacing and tell me what's wrong so I can help fix it.'

'I'll tell you what's wrong,' she finally said, fishing around in the black curls of her over-permed hair. She found her pair of goggles, pulling them down over her narrowed eyes and flung back the sheets on my bed. 'This is what's wrong!'

I looked at the sheets, expecting to see a slain cat or a half-skinned virgin but there was nothing at all except the wrinkles from my previous night's sleep. 'What? I don't see anything.'

She stormed over to the heavy drapes on my window and violently pulled them closed. With the room plunged into relative darkness, she flicked her favourite black light on and aimed it at the bed.

She'd nabbed the thing from an abandoned police station in Zone Five about six months ago, claiming it would be handy for cleaning up my many messes. She was right, of course, but it was still too funny watching her sweep the house.

Anyway, I glanced over at the bed sheets, specifically at the place where Mum was pointing. There was a large iridescent glow with pale blue highlights shining back at us from the centre of the bed. I was racking my brain, trying to think when I might have spilt something—blood, human body parts, anything.

'I haven't had breakfast in bed since you washed the sheets last,' I said, trying to insert some levity into the conversation. Mum wasn't buying it.

'It's not blood!' she shouted, her whole body quivering with rage.

'Then what's … ohhh.' I went dead silent. I didn't particularly want to think about the dried substance on my sheets and the disturbing thoughts undoubtedly flitting through my mother's head.

Clearly, Connor had left more of himself behind than just his underwear.

'Katie, please tell me this is just *special dreams* residue?'

Thank God the lack of lighting hid my flushed face; my wide eyes searched for a wastebasket to empty the contents of my stomach in. How was I supposed to answer that question?

'Uhh …'

'I take it this belongs to the boy who left his skid-mark jocks behind?'

'Um, gross, and thanks for the mental picture, Mum.'

'Don't get me started on the mental picture *I'm* getting just looking at this mess. How? Why? You know what, never mind. You are grounded.'

'Mum, I'm so sorry.'

She held up the black light, shining it directly in my face. 'Save it. I'm so angry at you right now I can't even look at you. You've been putting this family in danger left, right and centre lately. How do you know you haven't infected this boy?'

'We didn't really do anything.'

'That's because he was saving it all for the bed linen,' Mum muttered.

Kill. Me.

A vigorous knocking at the front door broke the tension.

Mum switched the black light off and threw open the curtains, allowing light to spill like nuclear waste back into my contaminated bedroom. The goggles magnified her eyes, only serving to exacerbate her angry expression. I glanced away, taking particular interest in the sisal weave of my bedroom's well-worn carpet.

Mum sighed and shot downstairs, leaving me to cower in the corner. I waited a further five minutes until I was certain she'd left me alone before re-emerging from the shell of shame.

The dreaded bed and crusty sheets were still in complete disarray. I debated whether I should hang them out the window and shake the shit out of them, but decided that the rear neighbours didn't deserve to see a body fluid decoupage today.

Instead, I quickly pulled up the covers and straightened the pillows. It wasn't an ideal solution given the company we were about to receive, but was the best I could do on short notice other than burn the bed.

Next time—if there was a next time—I was going to wrap Connor in plastic and introduce him to the wonderful world of Restraint.

Giving the room one final look over, I closed the bedroom door behind me and headed downstairs. A vigorous knocking at the front door indicated that the jig was up and the game was on. It was time for me to start playing the role of the innocent.

Mum and Dad were already greeting the sweep-over team, smiles fixed on their faces. Mum's bottom lip was quivering and tears were already welling in her tired eyes. Dad had more control, though a slight tremor in his hands suggested he was as nervous as the rest of us.

There were three members in the sweep-over team in total, all of them dressed in the same combat greens that the other guys from Zone Security had being wearing not more than an hour before. They looked so alike it seemed pointless to differentiate between them—brown eyes, greasy hair and midsections like a couple of off-road tyres. Clearly, these men didn't chase enough zombies. I wanted to slap them on the ass and see how long they'd run after me for.

Focus, Katie.

'Is this the girl?' Fatman One asked. I'd be calling him that until I knew better.

'Her name is Katie,' Dad replied.

Fatman One nodded. At least he'd called me 'girl' and not 'the suspected flesh-eater'. 'One of us is going to take her outside for questioning, if that's all right. The rest of the team will be searching the house, and after that, we'll look at drawing some blood. Results should be back within a few days, so we will have to remand Katie in custody until then.'

Not good.

'What?' Mum was still in a foul mood and clearly not to be messed with. I was glad she was on my side. 'No one said anything about taking our daughter away. She's innocent.'

'With the world the way it is now, ma'am, everyone is considered guilty until proven innocent.'

'But locking her up like a criminal? Is that what happens to members of the public who report zombie attacks?'

'Ma'am, your daughter violated Zone rules and is currently suspected of being one of the undead. Our hands are tied.'

'Blah, blah, blah, you can kiss my ass! Katie is not going to be hauled away like some—'

'Zombie?' Fatman Two answered, a wry look on his craggy face.

'She is not a zombie!'

Yeah, okay.

Dad slipped his arm around Mum. She collapsed against him, sobbing into his chest. Poor Mum. It had been a trying morning but I appreciated the support, even if she was lying through her teeth.

All three fat men finally made it past the threshold, threatening to burst through the cramped conditions of our entry hall. Like a bad crime drama, they all carried shiny suitcases and wore some form of magnified glasses, each pair sitting prominently on the ends of their collective, bulbous noses.

Fatman Three had his eyes squarely on me, his thin lips pressed into a hard line as he tracked each and every one of my movements. I started to think he might be a serious pervert, but then the gravity of the situation came crashing down upon me—keeping me in sight at all times was now this man's job.

I didn't blame him. Would you turn your back on someone you suspected licked brains?

Dad led a rather distraught looking Mum into the living room to calm down. Jack was undoubtedly pressed against the door, listening to the proceedings—not that he really understood the severity of the situation. I wondered if there was some way I could slink away, hide under the couch until this whole thing blew over.

Not likely.

Mum blew me a kiss. I made a show of catching it while

she mouthed how much she loved me, and then Fatman Three was signalling for me to join him. The other two branched off to start the sweep. Mum and Dad disappeared into the other room, closing the door behind them.

I followed nervously behind, my feet dragging on the hallway carpet Mum had miraculously managed to shampoo and vacuum just before the sweep-team had shown up. I couldn't help but assess the man's bulky bottom as we walked, my mouth watering at the thought of how many meals I could make out of that derriere alone.

Outside the sun shone brightly, a welcoming heat after the chill I had begun to feel running through my body. I'd made light of the situation but was now feeling exposed and vulnerable, like I'd been shoved under the proverbial microscope.

A beat-up white van was parked in the driveway, known to the general public as the 'Zombie Mobile'. Metal grill-work armoured the windows; extra security locks covered the side doors; but, it was the singular, hand-painted sign marking the vehicle as 'Zone Security'—okay and the machine gun bolted to the roof—that really spelled out the vehicle's function.

They obviously didn't take chances. And with over three-quarters of the world dead or undead, overkill was a necessity. I was surprised that Fatman Three was allowed to be alone with me given the circumstances.

'Katie, I'm just going to ask you a few routine questions and show you some imagery.'

'Um, okay.'

Like I had a choice. I wondered what would constitute a right or wrong answer. For instance, if he showed me a picture of a half-eaten body was I supposed to say 'yum, yum' to tick the zombie box, or display a suitable amount of disgust for the human? I figured if I went too far in any one direction I'd be crucified, regardless.

Moving a couple of meters from the driveway, Fatman Three ordered me to stand on the spot. I was in perfect view of any still-existing neighbours, and those that lingered had big freaking mouths—not the *all the better to eat you with* kind, but certainly big enough to destroy any vestiges of social standing that I might have had in the local community.

Curtains were already parting in the Fraser house across the street, and since the school bus was due to roll up in approximately ten minutes, I was sure the flow of gossip from this disaster would soon lead to me being ostracised indefinitely.

'Can we do this inside?' I asked meekly, shifting from foot to foot.

Fatman Three shook his head. 'The whole point of this exercise is to expose you.'

'But I'm innocent. I don't think you realise what this is doing to my social life.'

He chuckled, unlocking the side door of the van and retrieving yet another briefcase. This was the first time he'd turned his back to me for any extended length of time without glancing constantly over his shoulder. 'Good answer.'

One point to me. Apparently, it was normal for teens to freak out about their social standing. Ridiculous.

Fatman Three was ready for me now. He'd set up a rolling camera, a contraption so heavily bundled in duct tape that I doubted whether it could actually operate. On a little folding table, he'd switched on a voice recorder and had a Flip File folder full of what I assumed were grotesque images designed to shock and excite.

'Okay. For the record, please state your name and age.'

'I'm Katie Palmer and I'm seventeen.'

'Good. Now, in your own words, can you please recount your actions this morning, providing times and as much detail on the location and events as possible.'

I gave him the full story, sticking as close to the facts as I was able, trying to make sure I followed Dad's lead from earlier this morning. I emphasised how important the marathon was to me, that I was a school track star, and that I had spent many mornings and afternoons training for the very event that had been recently cancelled.

I doubted that Fatman Three understood the concept of exercise and the importance of its role in my life, but he barely interrupted my spiel, occasionally nodding and adjusting buttons on the video camera.

At just after eight, the dreaded yellow bus pulled up to the curb, the faces of my peers pressed against the plexiglass windows like goldfish in a tank as they watched. They all knew what the ugly white van in our driveway meant. Previously, you'd be strapped into a straight jacket and carted away to the funny farm when a vehicle like that drove up; now, the white just meant that you were totally fucked.

'Katie!' Nikki shrieked through a gap in the glass and grillwork. 'What's going on?'

After swallowing down my nervousness, I twiddled my thumbs for a bit and debated my answer. I decided that the best course of action was to go with the truth and poke fun at events, praying that my friends considered it all just a big misunderstanding.

'They think I'm a zombie!' I shouted, practically shitting myself at my own words.

'A zombie?'

'Yeah.' I pretended to growl and stagger around, much

to the amusement of everyone watching. A couple of the boys from the football team whooped and cheered, clearly thinking it was all just a big joke. I couldn't have been more thrilled.

Then I noticed Trenton Debrovnic briefly press his bruised face up against the plexiglass, beady eyes watching, expression grim. He'd obviously copped another beating from the jocks, one which was soon to be repeated as he was roughly yanked back from the window and disappeared into the throng of curious teens. Poor guy.

'Miss Palmer,' Fatman Three said, a wave of his hand recapturing my attention, 'please pay attention. This is a serious proceeding.' He tapped the side of the video camera to reiterate his point.

'Sure, sorry. I'm just super embarrassed, you know?'

'Of course.' He didn't look like he understood at all, though there was a small smile on his podgy face.

'So, are you coming to school or what?' Nikki continued to shout.

I shrugged. 'I don't know, maybe after they're done throwing body parts at me for shock value.'

Another bout of laughter erupted from the bus and echoed across the empty street. Fortunately, the bus driver had a schedule to keep and decided that loitering in my front yard was not on the agenda. He pulled away from the curb with a hiss and a roar, Nikki hanging her hand out the window and waving as the bus disappeared around the corner.

That hadn't been so bad. I was still presumed innocent by my school buddies but that may have only been the calm before the storm. We were teenagers and ordinarily it only took a few seconds for one of us to turn against the other. I doubted, despite their levity, if any of those on the bus would ever sit close to me again.

Fatman Three dug through the portfolio of pictures that lay on the collapsible table beside him. I figured we were about to play word association games, perhaps in an attempt to stir my appetite. I was still imagining barbequing his butt, so I really needed to focus.

The first picture he showed me was of a baked apple pie. The image did nothing to whet my appetite but I could still remember how I used to enjoy pie, warm and fresh from the oven, with a good dollop of fresh cream on top.

'It's apple pie,' I said.

'And, how do you feel about apple pie?'

'I don't know. I think they made a movie once about a guy who liked to shove his bits into hot apple pie but that was back in the nineties, when my Mum and Dad were still cool. Now, if you'd show me a bar of chocolate you might have gotten more of a reaction.'

That was a normal response, wasn't it?

A picture of a car crash victim was next. Blood had spilt all over the highway and bits of flesh could be seen hanging from the mechanical innards of the vehicle. 'How about this?' he asked, eyeing me cautiously.

I narrowed my eyes, as if I was having trouble making out the details, then screwed my face up. 'Why would you show me that?'

'How do you feel about all that blood?'

'Truthfully? That's just horrific. I'm thinking about reporting you for even showing it to me. You do realise I'm classified as a minor, right?'

'Now, now, Miss Palmer. These are just routine questions.'

'That wasn't a question, that was just mean. I'm going to have nightmares over that photograph.'

'Frank!'

'What!' Fatman Three shouted, not even bothering to look away.

'Get up here!'

We both pivoted and studied the second storey window of my bedroom. No one seemed to be panicking; if anything, the voice sounded jovial. One of the other Teletubbies had found something that was clearly amusing.

Oh, shit. My diary!

'Wait here, please, Miss Palmer. I'll be right back.'

As if. Despite all effort to be cautious within the diary's pages, I sometimes said things I shouldn't. I didn't want my innermost thoughts being revealed to these jerks. So, I took off after him, taking the treads two at a time, surprised at how quickly he could climb the stairs when pushed.

I loomed in the doorway, feeling panicked, feeling reckless. Only afterwards I realised that it may have been a cheap trick. If I had nothing to hide, then I should have stayed on the front lawn. Instead, I was acting guilty, crowding into the room, my eyes frantically searching for the source of trouble.

It took all of two seconds to realise I'd overreacted needlessly. The other Zone Security guys were fawning over my exposed sheets, a black light quite similar to Mum's shining over the top of the covers. I began to back out of the room, face aflame, praying that none of them had seen me burst in.

'Get a load of this!' one said, pointing to Connor's messy patch.

'Is that what I think it is?'

Right. So, they weren't taking their job seriously at all. They were making fun of the two thousand dried sperm spread across my bed sheets.

Laughter erupted, Frank enjoying the show as much as the other two. A thousand inappropriate jibes about

9 9

teenagers rolled back and forth around the room, but they were quick to re-cover the bed sheets when they realised I was there.

Their laughter died as quickly as it had begun. A few mumbled apologies were thrown at me before they continued with the task at hand. While *I* was still panicking over whether they'd find my diary or not, *they* were remembering that I shouldn't have been up there to begin with. Again, suspicion filled the air.

'Miss Palmer, please go back downstairs.' Frank was annoyed, but I suspected most of his anger was directed at himself for allowing me to see such an unprofessional display.

'Sorry.'

'Why are you even up here?' he said, realising I hadn't just followed him because I'd been missing his company out in the front yard. 'What were you afraid we'd find in your bedroom?'

This did not bode well. And the padlocks still affixed to Jack's bedroom door were also a worry. I couldn't believe that Mum and Dad had overlooked that.

'Nothing.' I started shuffling again. 'I was just hoping none of you would find what you did.'

Frank gave me a very slow once-over, the corner of his lip curling in what I could only deem as disgust. 'It's not yours, is it?'

'God, no! What do you think I am—a she-man? That belongs to my boyfriend. Right before you got here, my mum grounded me for letting him sneak into my room a while back.'

Frank's face started to bloom into a reluctant smile. 'I remember when I was younger and used to pop in and out of my girlfriend's bedroom window. Of course, I didn't leave any evidence I was there but …' He paused, scratching warily at his chin. 'Your boyfriend does know where to aim, right?'

'So gross,' I commented, turning my back on him and heading downstairs. I was not having this conversation with a stranger. It was bad enough that everyone had gotten to search through my bed sheets this morning; I didn't deserve to be given the 'square peg in round hole' speech as well.

Static, like the rustling of old newspapers or bad TV reception, hissed from his pants pocket and abruptly ended the conversation. I glanced over my shoulder, watching as he fished inside his combat greens and pulled out an old fashion walkie-talkie. 'Go for Frank.'

'Frank, you still at the Palmer house?'

Two treads from the bottom of the stairs and Frank was playing shy guy, making an effort to turn away from me and cover his mouth so I couldn't hear. 'We're still conducting the interview and searching the residence.'

'You can stop now. We've found another body, and this time we've cornered the undead culprit.'

Frank played peek-a-boo with me over his shoulder. 'Are you saying that the Palmer girl is no longer a threat?'

Holy crap. There's no way I could be this lucky.

'We need to monitor the situation, but we've also found the remains of that high school teacher. The undead we're trying to neutralise had the body, so it would seem there's no reason to continue detainment of the Palmer girl.'

'Are you sure?'

Thanks for the support, Frank.

'Unless that girl could be in two places at once, there's no way she's our zombie.'

I couldn't wipe the massive grin off my face. What were

the odds that another zombie had stumbled upon Mrs Cook's body?

'I'll let the crew know to start packing things up,' Frank responded, looking not entirely convinced of my innocence. Clearly I hadn't credited him with enough intelligence. He studied my relieved expression.

'Meet us on Waverly Road, just past the exit to Zone Three.'

I guess that meant Mrs Cook had been carried about three clicks south from the marathon track and in the opposite direction. Why would a zombie collect one body, move it to another location, and then go after a fresh kill? Something was seriously off here, but I couldn't quite string it all together.

'Roger that.' Frank slipped the walkie-talkie back into his combat pants, his gaze still on mine.

'I guess that means you're taking off now.'

Frank didn't respond, just kept on watching, judging.

'I can't say I'll miss you.'

'You got lucky,' he reminded me, a frown now plastered on his mug. 'Myself, I don't think you're one hundred percent innocent of wrongdoing. I'll be keeping my eyes on you.'

'Don't you have a zombie to catch, Frank?'

He clicked his tongue and crossed his arms. I seemed to be having trouble amusing Frank with my antics. 'Like I said, Miss Palmer ... I'll be watching you.'

I was about to remind him that even after the outbreak watching minors for extended periods of time was still frowned upon by the authorities but decided to refrain from antagonising him further. At least they hadn't drawn my blood.

Instead, I nodded meekly and backed up against the wall,

and waited patiently for him and everyone else to get the hell out of my house.

Next step? Pray that Heather Rosenthal got chlamydia and died, which would be a quick end to the inevitable rumour mill she was undoubtedly spinning into overdrive at this very moment. It was only a matter of time before she'd paint me as a villain and turn the whole school against me.

I could tell it was going to be a busy week.

CHAPTER SEVEN

Dear Diary,

The saga of the semen-stained sheets continues. Mum ended up telling Dad soon after she found the stain. Having her yell at me was one thing; having Dad frown at me like I'd been moonlighting as a hundred dollar bang-bang girl was a little too much to handle.

He hasn't spoken to me since the sweeper team left, but made sure to strip my mattress bare and burn the offending sheets in the backyard. I doubt very much if Connor will ever be allowed to cross the threshold to this house again.

Nikki called last night. The kids at school are talking about Mrs Cook's death and my possible involvement. Nikki swears that no one actually believes I'm a zombie, but apparently Heather is putting forward a good case, telling everyone who'll listen that she saw me out near the marathon track with blood all over my hands.

She might have been the person in the powder blue car. Then again, she could just be full of shit and riding on the coat-tails of opportunity. Either way she's ~~fucking dead if she keeps at it~~ a giant toolbag.

The winter formal is, unbelievably, still going ahead. I thought with so many dead bodies around they would have cancelled it but clearly ticket sales are more important than the safety of our town's youth.

Ooh, I forgot. Zone Security caught the zombie who

supposedly found Mrs Cook and made a meal of that nasty bitch who ran what was left of the public library. He apparently dragged both bodies to the other side of town and was munching away happily, right up until they blew his brains out. I'm not sure who it was yet ~~but I doubt it was the one who killed Mrs Cook, since they were supposed to be female.~~ In the meantime, I'll still suspect Heather Rosenthal.

Katie xo

'd asked Mum if I could skip the bus ride into school this morning. Bad enough that I was going to have to face those accusing stares in class, but riding on the bus for an extra fifteen minutes with insensitive football jocks and the other curious kids looking on would be a new form of torture.

Mum didn't mind. I was still grounded and she was definitely still mad, but we were both supremely grateful for my acquittal. Frank was still undoubtedly keeping tabs on me, though, so I needed to be more cautious than ever.

'Are you sure you're going to be okay? You can go back next week if you want,' Mum repeated, equally worried that, for me, today was going to be shit.

'If I put it off, they're just going to keep talking. At least if I'm there and acting completely normal they'll eventually get bored and stop talking about me.'

'You're right,' Mum agreed, fingers clenched around the steering wheel. 'You're such a brave girl. I love you, Katie.'

'I love you, too, Mum. I'm sorry I keep causing so many problems for us.'

'It's not your fault, it's that stupid soda company. If it was still possible to litigate, I would have sued the hell out of them.'

I nodded sagely. 'It's a bummer that they're all dead, I guess.'

'Everyone is dead or dying, Katie. I'm just so sorry I couldn't protect you from that.'

I swallowed the thick lump welling in my throat. Mum had a few stray tears running down her cheeks, which made it difficult to ignore my own. 'Aren't you glad you're a bloody vegan?'

She laughed, and licked away some of the salty tears that touched her lips. The rest she swatted away with the back of her hand. 'Yes, I suppose I am.'

'You would have hated being a zombie,' I said, prodding her in the ribs in an attempt to broaden the reluctant smile on her face. 'You know … all that meat.'

That did it. Mum's tears evaporated into laughter, filling the lines of her face with the brief flirtation of warmth. 'Oh, Katie,' she chuckled, speaking no further as we pulled up in front of the school and Zone Security closed the barbed wire gates behind us.

'I'll catch the bus home, Mum.'

'Are you sure?'

I shook my head. 'No, but like I said …'

'Okay, honey, but if you need me, ask the school to call.'

'Sure thing.'

I didn't look as Mum drove away. Instead, my eyes were fixed on the school's front doors and the patrolling members of Zone Security walking the perimeter. They watched me almost as closely as the loitering students hanging around the front car park did.

I took a deep breath. I'd expected this level of scrutiny but was unprepared to be the centre of unwanted attention. No one was pointing fingers, exactly, or whispering hurtful words under their breath, but their watchful gazes said these were early days. I wondered if they were worried I might eat them if ill words were spoken.

Perhaps I would.

I pushed on, and trudged up the front steps and into the cool corridors that followed. My locker hadn't yet been repaired but someone had modified the front since I'd last slammed it closed on Friday afternoon. The word 'flesh-eater' was scrawled across the front in red marker, just in case I forgot.

I ignored the insult and decided to use my anger in a productive manner. My fist found the dented right hand corner, and the busted metal compartment easily sprung open, especially for me. Smiling, I fished out my English books and Biology handbook, trying to ignore what I knew was a small crowd of onlookers gathering behind me.

'Hey, Katie,' Nikki chirped, sliding in beside me and opening her own locker. 'Why weren't you on the bus this morning?'

'I missed it.'

'Pity. Justin missed the bus this morning, too, and spent four blocks running after the bus before the driver realised he wasn't a zombie.'

'I guess everyone's under suspicion these days.'

Nikki tossed some books into her backpack and then slung an arm around my shoulder. 'Well, I don't believe for a second that you are one of *them*.'

'Your support means a lot, chika. Do you think you can get everyone else to stop staring at me like I'm going to unhinge my jaw and swallow them whole?'

Nikki cackled. 'I think some of the boys might like that.'

I shook my head, closing my own locker. 'Get your head out of the gutter, Nikki.'

'What?' she said, feigning innocence. 'I'm just saying that—'

'Yeah, I know what you're saying.'

'Come on, let's go to class,' she said, dragging me down the corridor between the gathering throng of people, who began to part around me like the biblical Red Sea before Moses. 'Who cares what these people think? Zone Security have cleared you, they've found the real culprit and—'

'Do you know who the zombie was?'

Nikki nodded vigorously. 'Someone told me it was that creepy guy with the dreadlocks that owns the video store in Zone Three. Apparently, they found a bunch of dead bodies in a chest freezer in the back room.'

'Wait, he was storing the bodies?'

'That's what I heard.'

'But zombies just eat people; they don't save them for later. The flesh has to be fresh because once it starts to decay it's no good.'

Nikki dropped her arm from my shoulder, her excitable face beginning to droop. 'How do you even know that?'

I pulled Nikki close again, tucking my arm through hers and not giving her a chance to doubt. I plastered a grin on my face and said, 'I've told you this before. YouTube!'

She laughed, her skittishness melting as we slid into the comfortable rhythm of our usual day together. We discussed a few other menial topics as we careened into class, taking up seats at the back of the room to avoid the ongoing stares of students too chicken shit to come up and actually talk to me.

Before the teacher entered and made us read something lame—like a book—I skirted back around to the zombie topic again. 'So, anyway,' I whispered, interrupting her as she recounted the harrowing tale of Justin's five mile death-run, 'what happened to dreadlock guy from the video store?'

'Oh, right,' Nikki said, frowning. 'I heard they blew his brains out.'

'So, who else was in the chest freezer?'

'No one we know,' she whispered conspiratorially. 'But there were a lot.'

'Were they eaten?'

She shrugged. 'I don't know.'

'Where did you get your info?'

'Taylor,' Nikki murmured, nodding her head in the brunette's direction. 'Her dad is a member of Zone Security. Apparently, he said that they think this guy was the culprit for all the murders now.'

'They *think*,' I scoffed, rocking back in my seat. 'That's reassuring. They have no problem blaming me because I found Mrs Cook and—'

'What the fuck!' Nikki shouted, the entire class turning in our direction. 'You never told me that.'

'Shhh!' I hissed, rocking back under my desk, and slapping her on the shoulder. 'Keep your voice down.'

'You have to tell me everything!'

'Will you stop yelling? Everyone's looking.'

She crossed her arms in front of her ample chest and leant back, levelling her eyes at me. 'Spill.'

It took the rest of class passing notes and small, unnoticed snippets of whispered conversation between us before Nikki got the picture. I didn't tell her about my zombie stalker or that Mrs Cook and I had had a good old yarn before she'd kicked the bucket. I did tell her about the car I saw, though, and that I thought the unidentified driver seemed to be following me, and that was why I'd admitted to being out running.

'Ooh, I bet your parents were totally pissed off with you.'

'They're more upset that Connor snuck in to my room during the lock-in.'

'They found out?'

Images of flaking white sheets flitted through my thoughts. 'Um, yeah. Connor left his underpants behind.'

Amongst other things.

'Did you guys …?'

'No,' I snapped, shooting her an annoyed look. 'You know I'm saving myself for Chris Hemsworth.'

'Ewww!' Nikki muttered. 'That guy is like a hundred years old.'

'He is not.'

'Didn't he get eaten?'

I shrugged. 'I'd do him, even if he was a zombie.'

'That's sick,' Nikki chided, shaking her head at me. 'Something is clearly wrong with you.'

Wasn't that the truth?

* * *

Biology crawled by. We were supposed to be studying osmosis or some crap like that, but instead we were having a few minutes of silence in remembrance of Mrs Cook, followed by group therapy. Every student had something nice to say about her. I was still a little filthy about the low grade she'd given me for my meringue, but I dug deep, remembering that her dying thoughts had been of keeping me safe.

Connor was also in Biology, but I hadn't seen or heard from him since Zone Security had begun their investigation. I had no doubt that he had heard of my predicament and thus concluded that our relationship was now over.

A few of the football jocks, however, thought my zombie experience was a big joke. One even slapped me on the back when they saw me sitting on my own at a lab bench, thanking me for yesterday's entertainment. I'd been so caught up in their levity, stoked that I hadn't been completely ousted by school society as a whole, that I didn't immediately notice Connor when he walked in.

Heather was right on his tail, whispering poison in his ear. She grinned lazily at me. I really wanted to tell him that he had a lying whore clinging to his back, but I was too ashamed to raise my hand. I couldn't stand the thought of him rejecting me up close.

Instead, I buried my nose in one of those lame-ass books I hated reading and continued to smile at the jocks next to me as their conversation eagerly digressed from zombies to boobs. Apparently I had nice ones, albeit small, but they'd thought it was their sleazy duty to tell me.

After a good forty minutes of avoiding eye contact with Connor and ignoring Heather's barbed comments, class ended. As I was leaving, I accidentally bumped into Connor in the corridor, my books spilling all over the floor.

'Why are you avoiding me, Palmer?' Connor asked, bending to help gather my belongings.

I finally looked at him, the magnificence of his blue eyes robbing me of breath. 'I-I'm not.'

'Yes, you are,' he chided. Connor ran an agitated hand through his sandy hair and helped me back to my feet. 'You've avoided looking at me all day. I thought perhaps you didn't like me anymore.'

'I've been in class,' I answered, snatching back the proffered books from his hands. Did that sound like concern in his voice? Was he seriously worried that I still didn't want to swap spit with him?

'Look,' he continued, grabbing me by the arm and dragging me into a quiet alcove across the corridor. A few people stared at us as they passed, whispering under their breath, but we ignored them. 'I don't think you're a zombie, Katie.'

I rolled my eyes, clutching my books tightly against my chest. 'I don't think I am either, and if you knew that you could've made an effort to talk to me in class instead of parking yourself next to Heather and buying into her propaganda.'

Connor squeezed my arm a little tighter. 'You were ignoring me. What was I supposed to do, embarrass myself in front of my friends?'

I glared at him, uncertain what to say but still hoping some grovelling was on the agenda. 'No, I just thought—'

'What? That I needed to apologise because you were too chicken shit to face me?'

'And have you openly reject me?' I scoffed, peeling his fingers away from my arm. 'No, thanks. Having everyone think I'm infected is bad enough.'

'I know you're undead, Palmer. You just aren't one of those crazy flesh-eaters. You may pretend to be normal for everyone else, but you don't have to play games with me.'

It was my turn to borrow Nikki's earlier exclamation. 'What the fuck?' I gasped. 'What are you talking about?'

'I know the truth,' Connor said quietly, gliding a slightly shaky finger down my cheek. 'Well, at the very least, I suspect.'

Thinking that this was probably some sort of trick, one of Heather's ideas to implicate me through self-admission, I feigned ignorance. I slapped his hand away, a look of what I hoped was abhorrence plastered across my face. 'Why would you say something so horrible to me after knowing what I've been through the last couple of days?'

'Because it's true.'

'Zone Security doesn't think so.'

'They're idiots.'

I moved to get past him, but he pushed me back, my spine

slamming against the row of lockers behind me. 'Let me go, Connor.'

'Not until you admit it.'

'That's never going to happen.'

The other students had now disappeared into their next classes, so Connor and I were now alone in the corner of a quiet corridor. We were at an impasse—no matter what he said or did I was not going to give myself up. I wasn't one of those stupid women in the horror movies who trusts the guy trying to get in their pants.

'Palmer, I promise that I just want to help you.'

I snorted and looked away, my knuckles white where they wrapped around the spine of my books. No one could really help me.

Connor crept closer. He kept one hand pressed firmly against the locker next to my head and snaked the other slowly around my waist. He pressed himself against me, his hot breath now whispering against my lips. Escape was possible but no longer my intention.

I tilted my head to look up at him, our eyes meeting across that limited divide. I searched his eyes for a hint of fear or trepidation but there was nothing but a brewing of molten heat. God, the way he looked at me made my insides melt.

'Connor, what are you doing?'

'I think you know.'

Before I could answer, he closed the distance between us and pressed his lips ever so gently against my own. His was a tentative searching, a very soft movement that I wanted to respond to but couldn't because he quickly pulled back again. 'I like you a lot, Palmer—I have done for a while. I'm not going to let a little thing like your illness get between us.'

I smacked a hand against Connor's chest and tried to shove him away, but he held fast, dragging me with him as we slammed into another set of lockers behind. 'Stop saying that!'

'Why, because it's true?'

'No, because you're going to get me killed.'

'You can't kill what's already dead.'

'Fuck you,' I muttered, detangling myself from his hold. 'Just stay away from me.'

I couldn't believe what I'd just told him. I wanted Connor in every way possible but had to protect myself. I couldn't put myself back in danger in exchange for puppy love.

Connor snapped his hand around my wrist, restraining me once more. I could have broken free, snapped his neck, and run off into the sunset a free woman. I didn't. I was too enamoured, secretly pleased that he might still want me despite my rotty bits.

'Let go of me,' I snapped.

'No,' he said, walking us backwards until I was once again wedged into a corner. This time he didn't speak, didn't ask permission, and didn't offer any form of explanation. He pressed his lips against mine with a savagery that bordered on the painful. Both his hands now cupped my face, his tongue exploring my mouth with ardent curiosity.

I was right there with him, hastily dropping my books to smooth my hands across the firm planes of his back, pressing my fingertips against his spine, pulling him closer. No matter how much I tasted or touched him, I couldn't seem to get enough.

Caution fading fast, I jumped into his arms, wrapping my legs around his waist in an effort to drag him as close to me as possible. He was groaning, my eager nearness driving his fingers downward. He toyed with the edge of my underwear, exploring the forbidden terrain beneath.

Yes. I did think about the dangers, and I did realise what

I was doing, but I couldn't seem to stop. Connor tasted like sunlight and his body felt like satin sheets. I kept my biting in check, gasping as his mouth slid to my neck, his teeth gently nipping at the flesh. I can't tell you what his hands were doing—even my diary wouldn't be rated high enough to describe those details—but we did break a few more lockers and set off the school fire alarm.

I grinned like a fool as, hand-in-hand, Connor began to drag me through the crowd of students and then out onto the school oval. Security was doing a fire sweep. I was still adjusting my skirt, but that small inconvenience had been worth it.

'We need to talk,' Connor whispered, mouth against my ear, his warm breath tickling my flesh.

'Oh,' I murmured, my mood crashing like a diabetic without a candy bar.

'No,' he said, squeezing my hand and kissing me on the temple. 'I just mean that we need to continue our earlier conversation. I have to explain why you can trust me. You'll never understand or believe if I don't explain how I know what you are.' He held up his hand, forcing me to silence before I could start protesting. 'Just promise me you'll meet with me after school so we can talk. Talk or something else.'

I shoved his shoulder, his cheeky grin hinting at exactly what else. 'I'm grounded, but I guess I already know how you feel about my parents' rules.'

'This is important.'

I studied his earnest expression. 'Fine. Where do you want to meet?'

'What about your place?'

'No way. You left your underwear on my bedroom floor last time and guess who found them? Mum.'

He grimaced. 'Okay, just be out the front of your place at about ten. I'll come by and pick you up.'

Reluctantly, I agreed, certain nothing good could come of diving deeper into my zombie past. Still, there was a big part of me that was supremely curious about what he would say. The other part? Just a horny teenager looking for a good time. Either way, nothing good could really come from this. I was getting in way over my head.

Again.

CHAPTER EIGHT

Dear Diary,

Two entries in one day—you are popular. This, though, will be the quickest entry in history.

1. ~~I'm thinking of using Roger the Shotgun on Heather and calling it an accident.~~

1. *Connor got me off in the corridor by the lockers—best use of class-time, ever.*

2. *Zone Three could really do with a new fire department. Turns out someone in the science lab dropped some chemicals over a Bunsen burner, and it wasn't my orgasm that started the fire. Disappointing.*

3. *I fully expect (despite the afternoon diddling and sincerity) for Connor to double-cross me and hand me over to Zone Security for indefinite detainment.*

Peace out.

Katie xo

S neaking out of the house proved to be easier than I'd thought. Dad had been keeping his keen eagle-eyed gaze on me since the bonfire ceremony in the backyard yesterday; however, he somehow failed to hear me climb down the trellis work and jump the rear fence, despite me losing one of my shoes on the patio and tripping over a garden bed.

Connor was supposedly meeting me out the front of my house any time now. Hopefully, he'd be a little stealthier about it than I'd been.

I commando dived over the side fence like I was waging war on the next-door neighbours. No one returned fire or made jokes about my exposed underwear—not that I expected them to. The house was abandoned, like so many others in this street, and now occasionally host to murder or used as a temporary shelter for the undead.

I headed for the front yard.

The house beside ours was eerily quiet, as always. With no light or whiff of life beating within its walls, the dank structure could easily have been mistaken as a breeding ground for evil. Festering zombies who'd managed to evade capture or death-by-barbeque tended to dwell in the area, coming out after dark to hunt through the back streets of suburbia.

I knew the ache of hunger burning within them, the desperation driving each onwards to murder; still, if I came face-to-face with one of those unwashed, herpes-covered miscreants, I'd have no compunction sledge-hammering their face in.

I straightened my skirt, pulled my knickers out of my butt, and picked up the pace, boldly stepping out and over the uneven footpath that led from the rear yard to the front.

An old gate crafted from an assortment of timber and wrought iron, blocked my path. It hung from rusted hinges, half of it drooping against the ground, the other half littering the uneven path in chunks the size of tennis balls. Amongst the debris were bits of smashed glass, a remnant of the once-whole front windows.

I quickly leapt over the wooden remains, my feet landing

almost soundlessly on the cracked concrete beyond. I gave myself a mental pat on the back and then restraightened my skirt again, brushing off any of the dirt still lingering after my nosedive over the fence.

Connor was already waiting for me in his car, with the head lights switched off and the engine lightly idling. He'd been smart enough to pull up in a driveway several doors down, rather than parking in front of my house.

I cringed as, very slowly and carefully, I lifted the door latch and slid into the cracked leather seat beside him. Still concerned about the noise, I took even longer to close the door, waiting until only a gentle click could be heard.

'Hey, Palmer. I'm glad you made it,' he said, smiling at me as though I was the very centre of his world.

My heart immediately turned to mush but I tried hard to fight it. I snorted, feigning annoyance despite the warmth spreading through me. 'Like I really had a choice. You're accusing me of some rather illicit behaviour, Connor.'

He popped the car into gear, flung an arm over the back of my seat and steadily reversed down the drive. The cheeky grin on those curved lips made me want to hop over the park break and start straddling him. I'd show him illicit behaviour.

'I swear that I'm not accusing you of anything,' Connor finally answered, speaking only once we were safely on the road and the lights of my parent's house had faded into the background.

'We'll see.'

We drove for a short time, sticking mostly to the security-sanctioned roads within Zone Two. Taking the backroads wasn't worth the trouble involved—we'd have to explain ourselves to the security stationed at each exit point, and outside the patrolled areas the festy kind of zombie roamed freely and hunted without prejudice.

I wondered if we were going to Connor's house. He lived around here somewhere but even though we'd attended the same school for years, I didn't really know that much about him.

I did know that Connor had lost both his parents during the initial outbreak, and that he now lived with his father's sister. I was lucky enough to still have my entire family—well, except Grandma now. Did I mention that?

R.I.P. Grandma.

'Are we going to your place?' I asked, remembering to buckle my seatbelt like a normal person would but about ten minutes too late. I didn't think flying face-first out the front windscreen was a big issue for me, as my flesh would quickly regenerate.

'No, I don't think that would be a good idea.'

'Afraid I might expose you? Afraid I'll see your wall of Justin Bieber posters?'

'You got me.'

My smile broadened. 'Okay, where are we going then?'

'Heather's uncle's beach house. She was going on and on about the winter formal today and just happened to mention that he's not living there at the moment because of the recent attacks in Zone Three. I figured that out there we'd be able to have the privacy we need to talk.'

I rolled my eyes. 'Aren't you worried about dumping us in the middle of the killing fields?'

'Honestly?'

'Yes.'

'No.' Connor draped a hand casually across my thigh and squeezed. That squeeze turned into a gentle kneading, his explorative fingers now rubbing circles over the exposed flesh just below the hem line of my skirt.

'Your blasé attitude worries me.'

'It needn't,' he joked. 'I've got you to protect me.'

'Me?'

Connor nodded. 'With your super strength and speed, I'm fairly certain you could take one of them on if they happen to stumble upon us, though the chances of that are low.'

I grabbed his probing fingers and peeled them away from my leg. 'You need to stop saying that.'

He placed his two hands back on the steering wheel, choking the cracked leather with his strong grip. The casual smile he'd worn since we'd left my place was now gone. 'It's just you and me, Palmer. We don't have to be careful about what we say to each other.'

'Says you,' I muttered under my breath, now regretting my decision to come. I blamed his boyish charms and that devilish smile, and I was almost sure it had nothing to do with his magic fingers and my easily parting thighs.

'Relax. We'll be there soon, and then we can take all the time we need.'

Ordinarily, I might have found that line sexy but there seemed to be an ominous undercurrent to his words that—in a sick way—now excited me.

I sat in silent contemplation. Clearly my protestations were falling on deaf ears. He believed I was a zombie as surely as the sun rose and set.

Ten minutes passed, with both of us lost to our own thoughts. I would have loved to get inside his head. I mostly wanted to be able to understand Connor's motives for pursuing me, but licking his brains clean was a side fantasy my zombified self couldn't help but ponder.

Connor turned the car down a winding lane. The tyres squelched along the muddy side-strip before finding traction on gravel, and then finally bitumen. Stubborn weeds and copious amounts of long grass grew over the boundary of the single-lane road. The foliage whispered against the sides of the car's paintwork as we passed, a faint scratching that sounded like tiny fingernails begging for entry into the cabin.

I rolled down the window; the summery scent of sea salt wove its way into the car's interior. The sound of water lapping against sandy shores in the distance was lulling, and I began to feel quite calm. My spirits were light, and a vast sense of freedom settled upon me, so close now that it seemed that I could reach out and touch it.

I stuck my hand out the window, allowing the feathery ends of the grass to tickle my palms as we passed. As the car moved faster down the deserted backroad, the tickling sensation became harsh and almost painful. I welcomed the sensation, a comforting reminder that a human part of me still existed and that I could still feel as I felt before.

Out of the corner of my eye, I noticed Connor occasionally glancing at me. He seemed so at ease, almost calmed by my presence. He smiled as I leant back against the headrest, enjoying the wind on my face.

Then we were slowing, turning off and then down yet another winding road. This one had enough potholes in its surface to rival that of an acne-riddled teenager's face. I hung onto the door handle as we bounced, occasionally ducking and weaving to avoid my head colliding with the rooftop.

No more than a minute later, we pulled up in front of an old timber-clad beach house. Heather had always made out that her family was rich. With its peeling paintwork, rusted mailbox, and pairs of weathered shutters that barely clung to their hinges, I'd expected something a little fancier.

A sweeping veranda surrounded the outside of the entire

house, marked by sturdy posts and flaking banisters. Despite the building's ramshackle appearance there was a liberal amount of outdoor space, so I could understand why Connor had urged Heather to let us use it as a party venue.

An exterior swinging chair rocked gently in the breeze, facing the rolling waves beyond. The solid chain it hung by creaked as it moved back and forth, as if controlled by the gentle persuasion of a ghost intent on enjoying the view and basking in the chilly, night-time breeze.

Connor killed the ignition and climbed out of the car. He shot me a brief, reassuring smile and took his time listening and looking around before he reached for the door handle. My senses were already on high alert but I appreciated the gesture. He didn't have anything to fear as I could neither smell, hear, nor see anyone close by.

I slipped out of the car before him. Chivalry was a forgettable notion when one's own personal safety was paramount. The number one time that zombies attacked was at night, when their victims least expected it.

Public toilets, car parks and fuel stations were high-attack zones during the initial outbreak. Even now, if you weren't in a building patrolled by Zone Security you were advised to walk around in pairs for protection. And always, *always* stay indoors at night.

'It's okay,' I said, and then thought better of it, wondering if my flippant manner might be mistaken for a further admission of guilt. 'Let's just go inside and lock up quickly, before anything comes this way.'

Connor nodded, taking my hand in his and closing the car door. With haste he led the way up the creaking steps and onto the veranda, the wood groaning under the assault of our combined weight. I understood now why Heather's uncle had decided to leave. Beautiful in its rustic charm, the house was still old and in bad need of repair. Cross-bracing had been placed with care across some of the filthy casement windows and was the only thing keeping the undead out.

Connor pulled back the flimsy screen door, which was designed to deflect the dusk dwelling insects of the sand and nothing more. He twisted the handle of the wooden door that followed and found it locked—no surprises there. Several more tries later and a clearly frustrated Connor slammed his fist against its surface.

'Did you really expect the house to be left open for you?' I asked.

'Well, no but—'

'Will this do?' I said, wandering over to the nearest window and sliding it open.

Connor grimaced, checking over his shoulder again. 'I don't feel right about leaving you out here alone.'

I rolled my eyes for the second time that day. 'Fine, I'll go first.'

'But what if there's something inside?'

'Connor—'

'Okay, I'm going in but stay close.' He leaned down and gave me a quick peck on the cheek, and then slid the window fully open. He popped a leg into the unbidden darkness beyond.

I watched as he melted into the shadows, his creaking footsteps the only evidence of his movements. Naturally, I didn't bother to wait for his all-clear. I slipped one leg over the window sill and started to feel for the floorboards on the other side.

My body was bent in two. I had just ducked my head through the gap and was reeling in my other leg when Connor appeared behind me, wrapped his arms around my waist and pulled me the rest of the way inside. 'I thought I told you to wait.'

'As if.' I reached back to close the window behind me and flipped the tiny lock back in place. Then I pulled the crumbling, sheer curtain closed, the veil of privacy it had provided virtually non-existent now.

Connor's hands tightened at my waist, his chest now pressed against my back. I tried to ignore the heat of his body, the smell of his soapy skin. 'We should talk.'

'We should,' I agreed, but there was something wrong with my voice. It sounded strained and airy, the hot breath that suddenly tickled my neck a major distraction. The tickling heat was closely chased by his supple lips, softer than tiny pillows and hell-bent on further exploration.

'Are we talking before or after?'

'After what?'

'You know,' he murmured, his fingers grazing my thighs and tracing a certain path to the edge of my skirt.

Oh, boy.

I was now standing at a virtual crossroads, craning to read the leaning signpost ahead—one sign pointed me towards losing my virginity, the other down the road to conversations best left unspoken. Thus far my mental feet were skipping down the yellow brick road of denial, chasing a flashing billboard that displayed a rather large picture of me with my skirt flung over my head.

The other direction marked a browning landscape dotted with mottled grey trees and naked branches. Ugly, fluorescent handrails prohibited veering off the chosen path, and reflective markers led directly to the flat, almost forgettable billboard in the distance. There was a picture of me as an old lady, surrounded by a million cats that I either ate for breakfast or kept for comfort. I couldn't tell which.

No wonder I was allowing Connor's creeping fingers to revisit the highlights of the afternoon.

'Stop,' I demanded, reluctantly capturing his hand in mine. He kept going. My breathing hitched as he continued to work his magic.

Why was I stopping him again? Common sense sucked balls.

'Why should I stop?' Connor murmured, echoing my own thoughts. He began to nibble one of my earlobes.

'Because I can't do this.'

'You did this afternoon, at school, in the corridor, with lots of people—'

'Yeah, I get your point. What I mean is that I can't keep doing this, and have you and I lead nowhere.'

Connor chuckled against my ear. 'We can rectify that.'

'No, we can't,' I said, spinning away from him and pushing him back. 'You don't understand.' Modesty dictated that I should straighten my underwear and pull my skirt back down, but foolish pride instead had me crossing my arms across my chest. I must have looked like a fool, but a fool who could stand her ground. I'd just have to ignore the sudden draft and lonely echoing between my legs.

'Of course I do.'

'How could you possibly?' I muttered, now pacing back and forth in the darkness. I let my hands slip to my hips, and then casually worked on inching my skirt down my thighs.

I wanted to explain to Connor that it wasn't my virginity preventing me from falling to the floor and letting him take that cherry; the thought of what else I'd be passing on— hunger, an unquenchable thirst, and, ultimately, death—was what gave me pause. Having sex with me was like catching the worst kind of herpes, and Connor double-bagging it wasn't going to help.

Connor sighed and reached for me again, his fingers sliding down my arm until he gripped my hand tightly in his own. 'I won't catch anything, if that's what you're worried about.'

My eyes snapped to his, my brow furrowing. I had to think of some sort of snappy retort, and quickly. Yes, deflect, don't admit to his suspicions. Otherwise, I might as well have painted a bright red target on my ass, bent over and took whatever was coming. 'Is it your goal to constantly offend me?'

Not particularly clever, but definitely the perfect aside to deviate from the central theme.

'Come on now, Palmer. Stop playing games.'

Okay, maybe not.

'This is why I brought you here, so we could be honest with one another.'

Round Two: Questions.

'By telling me I'm diseased?'

'No ... by telling the truth.'

Round Three: Deny everything.

'I don't know what you're talking about.'

'Yes, you do. I know exactly what you are and I want to explain to you why I know and why that matters. Respect me enough to not treat me like an idiot.'

I blew him a raspberry and went back to folding my arms across my chest, all defiance.

'Palmer, I know that you have a secret, and I understand why you are trying to keep it, but I have a secret, too. I need someone I can trust, someone who understands.'

I studied him carefully through eyes that were still narrowed, but I was listening now. He was serious, clearly struggling with some inner demon he planned on exorcising, whether I wanted part of it or not.

'I'm sick and tired of the isolation,' Connor continued, running an agitated hand through his sandy hair. 'I'm sick of knowing things about myself and other people that I have to keep hidden to stay alive.'

The troubled words pouring from his lips were intriguing. My frown deepened as my confusion grew, and yet I wanted to unravel his true intent. All we needed now was a campfire and some eyeball marshmallows and I'd be set for a great night of horror stories.

'Someone is after you?' I asked tentatively, not wanting to press him as hard as he was trying to ride me.

He shook his head. 'No, but they could be if they knew.'

Fuck. He'd suckered me in. Connor was flesh and blood—a tasty treat I'd put in a mighty effort to abstain. What was really going on and why did he need to put his trust in me?

I glanced around and found an old rocking chair propped against the wall in the corner of the room. I slipped into it—surprised and relieved when it didn't turn to kindling beneath me—and started to rock back and forth.

Connor followed suit, dropping like a sack of potatoes onto a dusty old sofa across the way that had been shoved against one of the heavily-stained walls. Powdered filth exploded from the mushy cushioning, so he wasn't surprised when I rejected the invitation to join him on the floral monstrosity. I actually liked this skirt I was wearing and didn't want to dirty it, but I also needed some distance between us.

I didn't have to sit twiddling my thumbs for long. Connor was in a hurry to get things off his chest. I was only marginally disappointed that it wasn't his shirt. I mean, answers were good, but abs were better.

'I know you're not comfortable talking about yourself, Palmer.'

An understatement. 'Whatever gave you that idea?'

'Hah. Palmer, *I* need to talk. I need someone to listen to me and hopefully understand what I have to say. Can I trust you?'

'I'm not sure. But, go on.'

'What if I just start back at the beginning?'

I shrugged. 'Connor, I'm listening.'

'I should have been just like you, Palmer. I should have become a zombie during the initial stages of the outbreak.' He held up a finger to silence me before I could emit yet another string of denials. 'I used to drink Popmade soda like it was going out of fashion, and I definitely threw back enough cans during the Olympic competition to catch the disease, but I didn't.'

'You were lucky,' I said, voice neutral. 'So many weren't.'

Connor shook his head, sitting forward on the sofa until his arms were resting on his kneecaps. 'I used to think that, too, but here's the kicker: I *did* drink enough to get infected.'

'But—'

'But I'm not a zombie.'

'How is that possible?'

He shrugged, a wry smile touching his lips. 'I have some sort of immunity.'

I swung back in my geriatric rocker, the wooden rim hitting the wall behind me and rebounding. I slammed both feet on the floor to still the movement and continued to study him carefully. 'Say that again?'

'There's something inside me that I cannot identify— maybe it's in my blood, maybe in my genes, I don't know. Whatever's different stops me from mutating.'

'But how do you know?'

'Experience.'

'Are you still drinking the contaminated Popmade soda?'

'No.'

'Then how do you know for certain that you can't be affected by it?'

Connor licked his lips, his head momentarily falling forward as he studied the floor at his feet. 'Well, you probably already know that my family was killed?'

I nodded, my expression suitably apologetic. I wasn't quite sure where this was heading but the conversation's destination seemed to be nowhere good. 'I'm sorry, Connor. This must be really hard for you.'

'Every day that goes by gets a little easier but I never forget. I never forget because I'm constantly reminded of it.'

'Because the undead are still out there killing people every day?'

'No, because I live with their murderer.'

'What?!' I shouted, jumping out of the rocker so I could join him on the couch. My skirt was filthy now, covered in a fine layer of dust, but that seemed insignificant compared to what Connor had just blurted out. 'Wait a minute … are you saying that your aunty turned and killed your entire family?'

When he failed to answer I prodded him gently in the side. 'Connor?'

'She didn't mean to,' he confessed, eyes still downcast. 'Everyday she gets better and better at controlling her hunger.'

'Oh my God, should that matter? How can you stand it?'

'She's the only family I have left.' Connor shrugged. 'Surely you remember what it was like in the beginning? Everyone seemed crazy; nobody understood what was happening to them. You were either turned, turning or dead. If you managed to survive you were lucky, but for how long?'

'But how did you escape? What stopped her from doing the same thing to you?'

'Oh, she tried to kill me, she really did.'

'What did you do?'

'I used a butcher's knife from the kitchen, hacked at her arms when she came for me, and finally had to slit her throat.'

I gasped and my hand flew up to my throat. I knew a cut throat wasn't a sure kill and that a potentially good feed would cure the injury, but the assault still would have hurt like a bitch.

Connor leant a little further forward, turning slightly so that I could see him lift the back corner of his shirt. His fingers skimmed smooth flesh until he found a raised area of rough skin and scarred sinew just above his hip. 'She tried to bite me right here,' he said, tracing the outline with eerie accuracy. 'But, apparently, I don't taste right. Something is wrong with me.'

I touched the exposed flesh, running the tips of my fingers over the scar tissue. 'But if she bit you ...'

'You'd think I would have become one of you. I mean, one of them,' Connor corrected when he saw the look on my face, 'but I didn't. Like I said, there's something a little different about me. I don't know what, but I'm immune from infection.'

'Connor, that's fantastic! Well, not that your gluttonous aunt took a chunk out of you, but that you're safe from this disease. Do you know what this could mean?'

He quickly pulled his shirt down, removing my hand from his skin as he saw that sparkle of hope in my eyes. 'Of course I know what it means. Why do you think I keep it a secret? I don't want to become some lab rat or a part of a government experiment just because they think they *might* be able to manufacture a cure from my blood.'

'But, Connor,' I said, regarding him sternly, 'you could save the lives of millions of people.'

'Maybe, maybe not. At least what I have now is a semblance of a normal life.'

'Really?' I chided, leaning away from him. 'You think this is normal? Do you remember what it was like to not feel afraid all the time?'

'Who are you kidding?' Connor said, his voice now as equally as agitated as my own. 'Who do you have to be afraid of? You're strong, and fast, and a deadly predator.'

'Yes, I'm a predator hunted by every human with a gun and a fucking pitchfork. If someone doesn't eventually blow my head off or stake my appendages to a wall, I'll have the Zone Authority to contend with. When they eventually discover what I am, I'll have the pleasure of having a collar slapped on me and be shipped off to the desert to rot. Eventually, even that would kill me!'

Fuck. The cat's out of the bag now.

Connor remained perfectly calm, his eyes now focused entirely on me. My eyes, however, were skimming the room for emergency exits, planning an escape route that would let me keep my limbs.

I shuddered, conflicted about how to proceed. Run, or take a breath?

'I first suspected what you were when you started coming to school smelling like soap and chemical cleaner,' Connor breathed, his voice quiet and calm. 'You avoid large groups if possible and almost always avoid eating in the cafeteria with everyone else. Most days you look like a runway model, with your luscious dark hair and dazzling obsidian eyes. On others I could see the hunger taking its toll as your pale skin fell victim to the disease.'

I went to say something, anything to divert the

conversation, but his fingers—warm and gentle and a comfort despite the fear licking at every one of my append-ages—closed around my own.

'My suspicion turned into certainty when you finally agreed to start training with me. No matter what I did I couldn't keep up with you, despite being fit and fast. Then, there was the smell.'

I moaned, yanking my hand free of his and burying my face in my lap. 'I'm so embarrassed.'

Connor rubbed a soothing palm across my back. 'Don't be. I barely notice your down days. I think you're doing well.'

'What does that even mean?' I grunted from between my fingers, head still pressed against my thighs. Clearly double-deodorising hadn't been enough.

I heard his breath catch, some strangled emotion momen-tarily trapping the words. 'You haven't killed your family yet.' Connor paused, hands still rubbing soothing circles. 'You haven't tried to eat me, despite how hard it must be to come so close to tasting what's right in front of you.'

I peeked up at him through my fingers and found a face filled only with compassion, not disgust. 'If you know what I am, and if you understand how hard it is to control my hunger, then you also must know what I have to do to keep fresh and maintain the image people expect to see.'

'Of course I understand. I live with a zombie and I see her struggle daily. She's overcome a lot of obstacles by eating animals, her mantra being, "If there is a will, there is a way".' Connor swallowed, shaking his head and then quickly replacing the pensive look on his face with a smile that seemed a wee bit forced. 'I'm sure you don't eat people to stay fresh.'

'Not on purpose.'

Connor's palm stilled on my back. 'Mrs Cook?'

'No!' I cried, leaping to my feet. 'Mrs Cook was …' I changed tact, having absolutely no idea how I could explain that whole episode. 'Look, yes, I have killed some people, especially at the beginning, but I try really hard not to let that happen anymore. I eat rats, hamsters, dogs, cats and even fucking pigeons. I just want to survive, Connor. I just want to be cured.'

'Cured,' Connor repeated, his voice now flat. 'Please don't do that.'

'Do what?' I barked.

'Imply that I could somehow help you rectify that. I've already told you how I feel—I can't be a lab rat.'

'Don't you think what you're doing is a bit selfish?'

'Selfish?' Connor said, now jumping to his feet beside me. He towered over me, his silhouette imposing in the darkened space. 'You think I'm selfish? What about you, Katie? If you want to start splitting hairs then even you have to admit that you put the members of your family in danger every single day.'

'Well, yes, but—'

'I also heard that you were being investigated by Zone Security. They don't do that without just cause.'

'Oh, please. Zone Security investigates anyone with a hungry look on their face within a six-foot radius of blood spatter.'

He snorted, turning his back on me.

'Where did you hear that, anyway? No, scratch that, I know exactly who you heard that from,' I snapped. Heather was obviously behind the poisoned whispering in his ear.

Connor spun back around, fixing me with a particularly cold stare. 'You do know that if they'd convicted you—which they could have—your parents would have been arrested. What would have happened to your little brother then?'

I shuffled backwards. Connor began to herd me into the corner of the room. I didn't stop until the rough wall of the beach house was pressed firmly against my spine.

I gingerly folded my hands behind my back, a little afraid of what I might do if he kept pushing. I was hungry, not starving, but I could eat. The thought of him tasting like toe jam did little to dispel the urge.

Just breathe.

What pissed me off most was that on some level he was right. I'd been keeping the darkest of secrets and forcing my family to do the same, just so I could pursue a relatively normal life. What real difference was there between me and Connor? We both had a secret we chose to keep under wraps for the sake of our own hides.

The only difference, damn it, was that Connor could possibly cure me!

'You're right,' I murmured, sliding my hands out from behind my back and placing them tentatively on either side of his hips. I waited for the moment when he'd push me away, but it never came, 'We're both selfish.'

Connor softened, melting at my touch and resting his palms on my shoulders. He inched closer, pressed his hips against mine. 'We're both still supposed to be kids. We weren't supposed to go through any of this.'

'No human is meant for this kind of life, Connor, but we can't dispute that we're the survivors.'

'And do you know what survivors do best?'

'Besides step over the fallen?'

He frowned momentarily. Connor was so close now that I saw his pupils dilate out to their limits, his blue eyes turned black in the darkness.

Strangely, I could see myself in those endless pools. They judged not my past indiscretions but measured me by the strength of my resolve. So I didn't protest, didn't struggle or decline the invitation of Connor's lips as they pressed against mine. In fact, I welcomed him into me, delighting in the taste of his tongue and the heat of his passion. But, most of all, I loved the scent of his acceptance.

'Can I ask you something?' I whispered against his lips.

'Sure.'

'Why me?'

'What do you mean?'

I playfully pinched his hip, disbelief marring my expression. His face wore an impish grin that meant he could see me perfectly well in the darkness. 'Come on,' I pressed, pinching him again until he fidgeted and angled himself closer still, 'I'm a zombie. Why the hell would you want to even be near me let alone mack on in an abandoned house in the sticks?'

'Mack on?' Connor laughed, the sound warm and rich and much more enticing than his cranky voice. 'Palmer, you may or may not know this but I've always had a little crush on you. Sure, I never made a move, but truthfully I thought you were too good for me. Plus, I'm not real good with rejection.'

I poked out my tongue. 'You dated the head cheerleader. That's gotta be a high-five moment for most boys on the football team.'

His hands slipped from my shoulder and headed south, his thumbs rubbing the material of my shirt just under the swell of my breasts. 'Heather is about as deep as a toddler's pool, and a gossip to boot. I was just biding my time while I waited for you to come along.'

I scoffed. 'That's total bullshit.'

'Fine,' Connor agreed without protest. 'I was hoping to get laid, but that doesn't change the fact that I've been crushing on you for a while.'

'Oh my God,' I groaned. 'You're still spinning it. In fact, my ears are bleeding listening to you crap on.'

'Okay, you got me,' he said as he grinned, quickly dropping a kiss on top of my shoulder. 'I've always thought you were hot, but I only really started paying attention when all this zombie shit started to happen.'

'Can you even hear yourself? You started liking me after I became a zombie?' I said incredulously.

Connor's grin widened before his lips playfully dipped to sample my décolletage, lingering long enough to make me squirm. It was all I could do to not collapse against him and surrender to his adventurous exploration under my shirt.

'Whoa, wait,' I said, practically panting as every part of my body seemed to come alive under his eager caress. 'Have you really considered what it is that you're doing with me?'

'Only one of my brains is working right now,' Connor mumbled, pressing the point quite literally to me.

'Seriously, Connor. I mean, if you think about it, you're a blooming necrophiliac.'

He groaned, throwing his head back to stare at the ceiling, clearly troubled. 'Are you trying to crush my boner? You're not dead, Palmer, you just have a disease. A disease I can't catch.'

'Still—'

'Look, don't get me wrong. There's no way I'd ever come near you with a ten-foot pole when you're oozing and falling apart. Stay fresh like you are now and I see no reason why we can't enjoy ourselves.'

In an instant I was back and standing at those crossroads again. Both billboards flashed with an urgency that bordered on desperation and depicted different images now.

On the first I was no longer clumsily clutching at a skirt recently yanked over my head. Instead, I was swinging said skirt in the air, reclining naked on the dusty sofa behind us with a satisfied smirk planted on my face. The only thing missing was a cigarette in one hand and an advertisement for Trojan condoms in the other.

The other billboard still contained an image of that sad, older version of my cat lady self. Additionally, now I was looking despondently over my shoulder at the other billboard, waving a white flag of surrender. An offhand shrug and a tiny caption at the bottom of the billboard only served to highlight the message: 'If you can't eat them, join them'.

I was seriously about to regret my choice, but was powerless to resist.

'What's it to be, Palmer? I've trusted you with my secret. You know that I'm harbouring a fugitive zombie at home. Do you think I'm going to betray you now?'

'You might,' I smiled, grabbing the front of his shirt and pulling him so that his eyes were now level with mine, 'but if you do you'll be sorry.'

'Is that a threat?'

I nodded. 'Put it this way—I don't care if you taste like boogers or Lady Gaga's upchuck, I *will* force myself to eat every square inch of you if you cross me. And it'll be finger-licking good.'

'Is that so?'

I giggled, my breath but a whisper against his lips. 'Try me.'

CHAPTER NINE

Dear Diary,

I know it's been, like, forever since I've made an entry but that's because I've been too busy having nonstop sex. Holy crap! No wonder everyone talks about sex; my body is like this weird computer with a million buttons you can push that make things explode. In my pants.

In case you're wondering, no, I haven't gnawed on any of Connor's bits despite him waving them around in my face. I have self-control and, I discovered, serious gagging issues. Who knew?

Anyway, there have been no new zombie attacks for days. Perhaps the freak from the video store was the culprit behind the attacks.

~~That still doesn't explain Mrs Cook's final words~~.

School's been going okay. Heather's still a fuckwit, but I can't see that changing. It really helps that I have Connor as a buffer, though.

Nikki and I have been keeping busy organising the winter formal and the Beach Bonanza. The teachers and administration think the student council cancelled the bonfire party but Heather, along with a host of other students, is determined to see it through. They're hoping to host it as the winter formal after-party.

Just what the world needs—an open-air gathering and drunk, unsuspecting teens to feed the natives.

~~Maybe I'll go native on the night and finally have a good meal ...~~

I haven't seen Dr Chalmers for a few weeks. Mum really thinks I need to go back to maintain some sort of order or sense of control. I've always thought seeing a therapist was a waste of time but some perspective might be good right now. With all the sex, my, uh, 'appetite' has increased.

~~I am a little sick of the pigeons. I'm super-proud of Jack's hunting skills, but I swear to God I'm going to shit feathers soon if I don't get a decent feed.~~

Katie xo

'Hey, Palmer,' Connor murmured, slipping his arms around my waist. He stopped to inhale my scent and then thought better of it, releasing me almost as quickly as the embrace had begun.

'Don't say it,' I muttered, digging around in my backpack for my can of air freshener. Supplies were a little light this week.

I found a quiet corner in the corridor and proceeded to douse myself, stopping only when Connor started to cough profusely.

'You need to eat something.'

'Tell me something I don't know,' I snapped, dropping the near-empty can back into the confines of my bag. 'A pigeon a day does not keep the festiness away.'

Connor snuck into the alcove with me but staying as far back as he could. Not that I blamed him. 'You have to slow down your training. You're exerting too much energy.'

'I don't want to stop training. I know they cancelled the marathon, but I'm the top athletics student in my class. If I keep flunking Math and Biology, I may need to rely on my sporting ability to get me a job when school's done with, as unlikely as that is.'

I liked that Connor didn't discount my reasoning or point out that the only athletic jobs left were lugging rickshaws in China. 'So what are you going to do about ...?'

'The smell?' I shook my head, genuinely without an answer. Mum and Dad had exhausted their supply at the local pet shops, and I couldn't keep preying on the neighbourhood pets for food. What I really needed was a body—alive, fresh and willing to offer up life and limb.

Couldn't really see that happening.

'Ughhh, what's that smell!' Heather said, sweeping around the corner and throwing an exaggerated hand across her mouth. 'Maybe Zone Security *should* have investigated further. You smell like the dead, Katie!'

'That's just your own breath blowing back in your face,' I retorted, spurred on by a burst of laughter from Connor's mouth.

Heather ruffled her short blonde hair, her eyes narrowing into angry slits. She blocked her nose again. 'You think you're so funny, don't you?'

'Not especially; you're just an easy mark. I'd say it's all that hair dye that's finally bleached the rest of your brains out.'

'Well, at least that way I'll know that you won't want to eat them out of my skull.'

'Oh, that's good,' I said, rolling my eyes. 'Did you think that one up all on your own? Gold star for Heather.'

'Make jokes, but I know what you really are.' Heather spat.

I tapped a finger against my chin and looked up at the ceiling as if deep in thought. 'Um, would that be super-hot, charming and intelligent?'

'All three,' Connor murmured, giving me an appreciative smile.

'Thanks, babe.'

Heather, annoyed that we were ignoring her, stamped her foot. Even though I smelt like roadkill and looked like that scary chick from *The Grudge*, Connor still only had eyes for me. 'Don't think I'm not watching you,' Heather continued, raising her voice. 'Everyone else may believe you were wrongly accused, but I saw the blood on your hands. I know you were doing something disgusting out at that stupid marathon track.'

My head snapped back in Heather's direction. I was no longer distracted by Connor or the previous conversation. I was now focused on silencing a blonde bimbo who had seen more than she should have.

'I ... what?' I finally answered. 'What did you just say?'

Connor's fingers brushed my side ever so slightly, perhaps his way of warning me to keep my anger in check and not push the issue further. With Heather, though, it didn't really matter whether I had it out with her here in the corridor or left her to spread idle gossip in the classroom. From the evil glint in her beady, green eyes, she looked to have every intention of bringing me down. She'd save this little gem for when it could hurt me the most.

'You heard me.' Heather placed a hand on Connor's shoulder, indifferent to the fact that he shrugged her away. Instead, she crossed her arms over her ample chest and stared me down with a purpose.

'You obviously saw wrong.'

'Then why chase after me?'

She had a point. I couldn't exactly tell her I'd thought she was the zombie who'd tried to finish off Mrs Cook. Admitting that would be like admitting Mrs Cook had died from something other than a video store attendant's bite.

'You see, I've been trying to protect poor, misguided

Connor,' she said, reaching out to stroke his arm but again meeting with rejection. 'I know something's not right with you, and that's why I followed you that morning. It's also why I've been watching you like a hawk ever since. I know the truth, and I think Connor is in danger.'

'And what exactly is the truth according to you?' Connor hissed, his voice tight and lips pressed into a thin line. His hands clenched into angry fists at his side, shoulders hunched forward. He looked like he might windmill her in the face with his fists at any moment.

I was all for that plan.

'That Katie Palmer is a zombie.'

Her voice was loud enough to carry to a few kids loitering in the corridor. With nothing better to do than doodle unattainable boy's names in their maths book and complain about teachers and their affairs, new rumours were undoubtedly already doing the rounds.

I seriously considered ninja-kicking her in the tits just so I could watch them explode all over her face. I'd never hated anyone in my life, but Heather was shaping up to be an exception. 'Be careful what you say,' I advised, checking my tone and stance. I'd been staring her down like a hungry vulture, and I didn't want to be the main character in the picture she was painting.

'Or what?' she challenged, placing her hands on her hips. 'Are you going to eat me?'

I took a moment to breathe. 'I'm not a zombie,' I said for like the seventeen millionth time that year. Shakespeare had once said something about protesting too much, but he'd also been English.

These days you couldn't trust the English. The Queen had been a fan of Popmade soda—for those first few days after the initial outbreak, the royals in Buckingham Palace had treated London like a buffet. Millions of people had found themselves packed into a sardine can of a country with a hungry old lady and killer corgis, all out for blood.

But, I digress.

Heather leaned towards me, making a dramatic show of waving some fresh air into the space between us. 'You can't be too careful these days, can you?'

'Starting false rumours could get me killed, Heather.'

She scoffed, backing out of the alcove and into the main corridor. She swept her arms out wide and took a minute to make sure there was enough of an audience to proceed. 'I'm more worried about you killing other people. Kind of funny that your Home Economics teacher wound up dead now, isn't it?'

'Shut the fuck up, Heather,' Connor interjected, slamming a fist against a nearby locker. 'You don't know what you're saying, and you're going too far.'

'Oh, I'm just looking out for the student body. Doing my bit to maintain public safety.'

'Come on kids, get to class!' Mr Gray shouted, suddenly appearing out of nowhere. He ushered Heather down the corridor with a polite shove and clicked his fingers at the other students close by. She shot a satisfied smirk at me over her shoulder, flouncing off and disappearing into her next class.

Mr Gray nearly walked by us, but stopped in time to notice Connor and I still huddled in the corner, staring daggers after the blonde reaper in the cheerleading uniform. He studied his wristwatch and shook his balding head. 'You're late, Miss Palmer. And, Mr Watters, I suggest you get moving before I card you for detention.'

'Sorry,' we mumbled, bowing our heads and making our way to class. We tried to ignore the pointed stares and continued whispers of the other students still loitering as we passed. Thankfully, Mr Gray was already barking orders at them, and once more seeing us all on our way to further education.

'This isn't good,' Connor muttered under his breath, staying close. 'Why didn't you tell me Heather had seen you?'

'I didn't know until now.'

'We need to talk about this.'

'Yeah, later.'

I left Connor in the corridor and followed Mr Gray into class. I had no idea how I was supposed to concentrate on Math now, but Nikki's warm smile and wave to me across the room seemed to lighten the burden.

*　*　*

'Hi, Katie. It's been a little while since you were here last. How have you been?'

I smiled weakly at Dr Chalmers. In truth, I wasn't doing so well. It had been weeks since I'd had a decent feed and my body was starting to show the signs, which made sense since I was basically living off of a diet of appetisers. I looked tired, sallow, and I was still a little on the nose.

The incessant sex had come to a grinding halt. Heather had been making my life a misery, and rumours ran afresh, with Zone Security back on the scene and breathing down my neck again.

Frank was virtually everywhere I looked—his lard ass was always in the rear view mirror, his bulbous nose constantly peeking out around the corridors at school. I'd been living off rats trapped in the roof at home, some pigeons, and a few toads I'd found hopping in the backyard. I wasn't crazy-starved but my stomach was constantly gurgling. I couldn't hunt because of Frank, and I could barely defend myself against the rumour mill.

I looked like a junkie and smelt like a corpse.

Even now Dr Chalmers was sitting back in her chair, her nose twitching as if trying to weed out a bad smell. I'd already positioned my chair as far away from her as was possible and refrained from making any sudden movements that might shift my odour-laden air towards her.

'I'm okay,' I finally answered, never really knowing what was safe to reveal.

Dr Chalmers sighed, crossing one of her slender legs over the other and leaning further back in her chair, perhaps in a desperate yet socially-acceptable attempt to get away from me. I wondered if I should tell her that I had some serious gas issues at the moment.

No. Best to pretend nothing's wrong.

'You don't seem okay. Has something happened at home?'

'No.'

'Katie ...'

'I can't really talk about it.'

'Then perhaps you might want to talk about the Zone Security investigation into your possibly status as a zombie?'

'How did you hear about that?' I said, shuffling uncomfortably in my seat, though I had my suspicions.

Dr Chalmers tapped her pen against the pad sitting neatly in her lap, and then looked up. She brushed a stray piece of auburn hair behind her ear and then folded her hands tidily in her lap. 'Your mother had a word to me about the whole incident over the phone. She's very concerned that it may be taking a toll on your health. Your mum also said you're not sleeping, that you're barely eating.'

'The eating thing is not by choice,' I muttered under my breath.

'I beg your pardon?'

'Nothing.'

Dr Chalmers quickly wrote something down, probably 'possible anorexic' or 'self-harmer'. That would certainly explain why her eyes kept travelling the length of me whenever she thought I wasn't looking. Funny how people had to label you as something. I couldn't just be Katie Palmer; I had to be Katie Palmer, anorexic zombie, or Katie Palmer, nutritionally deficient and filled with avoidance issues.

I supposed to a professional labeller like Chalmers that did have a nice ring to it.

'You look so tired, Katie. Why don't you just tell me how you are feeling? It might surprise you how good it feels to get a few things off your chest.'

Like my bra? The underwire was itching the crap out of my flaky skin. It was all I could do to stop from squirming, which would push the smell further around the room. I studied the floor at my feet instead, wishing I was anywhere but here. I needed to hunt, I needed to run. I needed some fucking meat, not a bloody therapist.

I giggled, amused by the image. Actually, a *bloody* therapist would probably fit the bill quite nicely.

God, I'm hungry.

'Is something amusing?'

I shook my head and looked back into her cold, brown eyes. For a therapist she really didn't show much compassion, just sort of stared me down until I felt compelled to say something, anything, to get her to look away. 'I'm just upset, I guess.'

Her demeanour softened somewhat, her porcelain brow crinkling with what I perceived to be manufactured concern. 'Talk to me, Katie. I really think I can help, even if all I can do is listen to you vent.'

'I'm innocent, you know.' *Of most things.*

'Of course.'

'I just feel like I'm under constant scrutiny. If it isn't Security keeping their eye on me, then it's people at school going out of their way to make my life miserable.'

'It's an unfortunate situation that you can't necessarily change. If you are innocent then Zone Security will eventually realise this and leave you alone.'

'*If* I'm innocent?'

She waved a hand at me to dismiss the remark. 'I simply meant that these things take time, and *when* you are acquitted the pressure on you and your family will lessen.'

'That fact is not going to stop me from being picked on at school.'

'I'm so sorry to hear that you are having a hard time. Kids can be cruel and unforgiving.'

I nodded, feeling the slight welling of tears at the corners of my eyes. 'It's just hard to keep hearing the same rumours again and again and to keep getting treated like I'm some sort of infectious disease.'

'But you are.'

'What?' I snapped, eyes wide at the accusation.

'Well, to them you are,' Dr Chalmers corrected, making fresh notes on her pad. 'Teenagers have nothing better to do than gossip and heed the fiction of those they regard as being superior. It gives them a sense of purpose and diverts the ugly limelight away from their own insecurities.'

'I know that,' I mumbled, settling back into my chair again. 'But it hurts to be made fun of, and now even my best friend is starting to doubt me. I just wish she'd stop listening to Heather's slutty mouth.'

Dr Chalmers raised a singular eyebrow. I thought she might pull me up on my language like my mum would have, but instead she said, 'So there is a ringleader involved in these rumours?'

I nodded. 'Yeah, Heather Rosenthal. She's been following me around, whispering behind my back, and telling everyone that she saw me with blood all over my hands.'

'And why would she do that?'

'Because she hates me and because she's a stupid slut with a cranky vag—never mind.'

'Katie …'

'Sorry. I'm kind of emotional right now.'

'I can see that,' Dr Chalmers murmured, her eyes darting between her notes and my stressed features. 'But I'm glad to see that you're at least talking today. You very rarely open up, so to have you speak is refreshing.'

'I'm glad I've made you happy,' I muttered.

Dr Chalmers ignored that. 'Have you kept up with writing down what you can't seem to speak out loud?'

I shrugged. 'On and off, when the mood takes me.'

'Do you find writing regularly about the things that make you happy or that writing about problems like the Zone enquiries gives you a sense of peace?'

I screwed my face up. 'It's just a diary.'

'Yes, but do you?'

'I guess so.'

Dr Chalmers moved forward in her chair, her elbows perched precariously on her slender thighs. She'd tucked the notepad somewhere in the upper folds of her over-starched trousers. Taking a deep breath and carefully revealing a gentle smile, she said calmly, 'Would you perhaps be open to letting me read it, since you're not particularly verbal during our sessions?'

I was taken aback; my diary was a very personal thing. Granted, it was filled with an abundance of blacked out sections, areas where I'd been a little too passionate when discussing my 'alter ego' but there was still a risk associated with allowing anyone near the scent of something so suspicious.

'Um, yeah, no.'

Dr Chalmers pursed her lips slightly as her expression hardened and then faded back to one of neutrality. 'I apologise if it seems like I'm prying. I really only want to help.'

'I know,' I said, offering her a smile. 'It's just that there's some fairly personal stuff in there.'

'Death threats directed at Heather Rosenthal, perhaps?'

I cackled at her attempt at a joke. 'Yes, that, and a few things that would make my Mum blush and my Dad ship me off to the Amish for reformation.'

Dr Chalmers smiled knowingly. 'You're referring to sex?'

I was pretty sure my face had just exploded into a ripened berry colour of embarrassment. I couldn't even answer her, only shrug and stare back down at my feet to avoid the limp smile attempting to lift the corners of my mouth.

'You don't have to be embarrassed, Katie. I'm your therapist. Whatever you say here is strictly between us.'

'I know that.'

'So, talk to me.'

Why was she always so pushy?

'No offence, but I don't really want to give you a play-by-play description.'

Dr Chalmers chuckled, the first real sign of levity she'd ever shown in our sessions. I was glad to see that she could do other expressions, rather than just frown or stare at me stoically. 'Katie, although I'm sure your experience would end up as drugstore fiction, I'd really rather you left out the finer details of your trysts. But you are welcome to ask me any questions that you may have. I know that parents can sometimes be difficult to approach.'

'That's okay,' I said. 'We have Sex Ed class at school. I'm fairly certain I can bag a banana and recognise genital herpes for what it is—gross.'

'That's good to know.'

A few uncomfortable seconds of silence passed between us. 'Can I go now?'

'You're always so eager to leave, Katie. We still have a few minutes of our session left.'

'Yeah, I know, it's just that I have some things to do.'

'Like plot revenge against Heather Rosenthal?'

A ghost of a smile touched my nervous lips. 'Naturally.'

She gestured to the door behind me, another miraculous smile fanning across her fuchsia-stained lips. 'Then you can go.'

Well, *I'll be.* I could honestly say that had been the first session I'd had with her in which I'd felt a semblance of understanding towards my plight. It was also the first time ever that I thought, perhaps, I might actually be starting to like the uptight, pen pushing Dr Chalmers.

Who would have thought?

CHAPTER TEN

Dear Diary,
Mum and Dad are making me sleep in the backyard. We're
calling it 'camping'. At least three times this week I've tried
to break through the locks on their bedroom doors to chase
a midnight snack. Jack has taken to sleeping with Mum and
Dad, and Mum and Dad have taken to sleeping with Roger.
~~Thankfully, I'm yet to swallow a bullet, but I've been eating~~
~~nothing but toads and a few rats so I'm fairly certain my luck~~
~~will soon run out.~~
I haven't been to school for a few days. Heather spray-painted a
new slogan across my locker, and the teachers have complained
to my parents about my personal hygiene. I have no idea how
I'm going to bounce back from this socially. I was crazy to think
that I could live a double life and still be 'normal'.
I have to do something, and soon.

Katie xo

I studied the crackling flames, letting the warmth they provided soak through my skin and into my bones. Inside, I could hear the sounds of the TV and my family laughing. They were watching old movies and TV show re-runs. There were no new TV series or movies made anymore except for the amateur YouTube enthusiasts producing shaky videos on the intricacies of zombie killing.

I imagined my parents snuggled up on the warm couch, eating popcorn and ruffling Jack's hair. I wondered if they missed me, if a part of them felt guilty for banishing me to the backyard while they enjoyed family hour without me.

I sniffed under my armpits and almost passed out. Nope, there was no way in hell they missed that. I really needed to eat.

I got up from beside the fire, crept around the side of the tent and wandered carefully over to the fence that faced our front yard. Instead of sticking my head above the palings, I peeked through the gaps next to the rickety gate, and saw Frank's unmarked car parked on the opposite side of the street. Lard-ass was shoving doughnuts into his gob, occasionally taking a sip of coffee as he glanced back and forth between the house and his meal.

Frank had a hunch and had stuck close. He was like a festering butt pimple that I just couldn't seem to squeeze. I was starving and needed to hunt; Frank was the only thing currently standing in my way.

I tapped a finger against my chin, debating with my conscience. Animals had been scarce during previous hunts. I suspected that was due to my recent competition in the area and that old adage—a greedy fucking zombie has no intention of sharing. Of course, now I was struck with a moral dilemma. Did I try to escape Frank's nightly vigil, or did I directly deal with a problem preventing me from leading the normal life I coveted?

Decisions, decisions.

My growling stomach answered for me.

I spun around and sprinted across the backyard. When I reached the fence on the opposite side of the house, I peered through the palings again and waited until Frank was distracted by his doughnut. Then I leapt up and over the six-foot fence and into the neighbouring yard.

There were no living neighbours on either side for three houses in either direction. My only obstacle to food would be the Fraser's house across the street, which happened to be right in front of where Frank had parked.

As usual, the curtains were open so that nosey bitch could keep an eye on the entire neighbourhood without ever having to set foot outside her house. I couldn't see her pacing in her nightgown and rollers, or stroking the little French bulldog I'd tried to barbeque weeks earlier. Perhaps she'd lost interest in the affairs of others?

I cackled to myself and then straightened, realising I was about to pull some serious shit. I needed to get my head back in the game.

I started forward through a tiny yard that had been very tidy once, tended to by a lovely old lady called Hester. She'd passed away from a heart attack right after the outbreak. After taking one look at the flesh-fest in her front yard, she'd keeled over in the living room and was dead a short time later. I'd been lucky enough to find her. Her recently deceased flesh had been enough to sustain me for almost two weeks.

Yes, I sure missed Hester.

Now her garden was overgrown, the roses that once curled around trellises were dangerously out of control. Thorns nipped my flesh at every opportunity but I ignored their little stabs of pain, continuing through the maze and towards the next fence.

When I was at least three houses down from my own, I found myself suddenly bathed in the harsh brightness of a sensor light that one of the families still living on our street must have installed. I quickly ducked into the shadows and headed for their front yard.

Keeping close to the walls of the house, I checked back

down the street and towards Frank's car. He was still sitting in the driver's seat, occasionally glancing up at my darkened bedroom window.

Crossing the street posed the greatest risk. Although I was fast, I had no doubt Frank would catch a flash of something in his peripherals or side mirrors.

I sat, perched by the brick letter box for what felt like an eternity. Then, when I saw Frank lean forward in his seat, perhaps bending to adjust the height of his chair or change the radio station, I sprang forward.

I sprinted across the open road and practically dived into some of the nearby bushes. I lay silent, not moving a muscle. For a few further minutes I listened intently to the sounds of my neighbours, relieved to not hear the start of an engine or the opening of a car door.

I crawled slowly from behind the bushes, not bothering to pick the debris from my hair or brush down my clothes. I'd be burning my current outfit by the time this night was through to get rid of evidence.

Retracing my earlier movements, I crept carefully and quickly through the neighbouring yards until I was crouched by the fence next to the Fraser's house. Inside, the lights were on but there appeared to be no movement. Flickering shadows in the living room suggested that the TV was on, but I couldn't hear it, not even this close to the premises.

Checking in Frank's direction, I slipped over the fence and commando rolled underneath the nearest window. Taking my time, I pulled myself up slowly, wishing I could flatten the top of my head so only my eyes were visible when I looked over the window sill.

Mrs Fraser's varicose-covered legs came into view first. They hung limply over the edge of an ottoman, her arms following suit. At first I thought she might have been dead, given the unlit cigarette dangling from the edges of her lips and the angle of her head as it rested on the cushioning.

On closer inspection, it soon became clear that she was either passed out or asleep. I was going for option one since there was an empty bottle of Wild Turkey next to her chair and a tiny trail of vomit on her chin. And an even bigger puddle on the floor.

I started wondering why I shouldn't put her out of her misery and devour her instead of Frank, but she looked so pathetic I decided I couldn't. She was a pile of skin and bones, a drunkard. I decided she could be my backup plan if there was eventually no one left to eat on the planet.

I watched her a few minutes longer, noting that her French bulldog was huddled in the corner of the room and fast asleep on his bedding. It was safe to assume those two wouldn't be witnessing any crime tonight.

I started to creep back along the side of her house and edge my way closer to the front yard. As I said, Frank's car was parked conveniently in the Fraser's driveway so I wouldn't have to go very far to keep an eye on him. My plan was simple: Eventually the fat guy would need to pee after consuming that much coffee. That would be my time to pounce.

The trick was to make sure suspicion didn't fall upon me, which was why Frank would not be found in the driveway across from my house. And, since he was watching over me as more of a hobby rather than as a security sanctioned assignment, I doubted if anyone would come knocking on our door to ask questions.

It scared me how organised this murder was turning out to be.

I ended up setting up camp on the other side of the house.

I wanted to be on the passenger side of the car, knowing that if Frank did leave he wouldn't go far and wouldn't be long. The time was well after midnight, so I very much doubted that he would knock on the Fraser's door to use the bathroom. All I had to do was wait.

About three hours in, I started to get pissed off. I'd been lying down on the grass, my head supported by the palm of my hand, watching and waiting for the Olympic champion of bladder control to step outside of his vehicle. Regular checks inside the house ensured that Mrs Fraser and her tasty bulldog were still fast asleep. All I could do was lounge around in her front yard and wait for my meal ticket to take his next whiz.

My other hand picked at the dew-covered blades of grass, shredding them with my fingernails and scattering them to the wind. One of my legs had gone to sleep, and my hip was killing me where I was laying on what would later turn out to be quite a chunky piece of rock.

I really hoped that Frank was pleased with himself and his—

Yes!

The locks on the doors disengaged, the click of one handle opening like a dinner bell. I tried scrambling to my feet but pins and needles had taken hold, and I wound up dragging my sorry ass into the shadows of the shrubbery near the fence instead.

I watched as Frank slowly pushed open the car door, taking his time to study the street before he stepped out into the cool night air. He stretched his arms gingerly above his head, and then slowly and quietly clicked the car door closed behind him.

He surveyed the street once more; he was a cautious bastard. I certainly respected his tight hold on life and the tenacity with which he fought to protect others. I almost felt guilty because of what I was about to do.

Almost.

Once Frank was satisfied that the coast was clear, he turned and rounded the car and headed in my direction, the zipper of his pants already making acquaintance with his fingers. Not until his pants were headed south and his pecker had popped out to say 'hello' did he realise I was standing almost on top of him.

He knew. I could see it in the wide gaze of his tired brown eyes. Frank knew he was done for. He didn't even bother reaching for the gun stashed in the back of his sagging pants or bother to cry out for help; he merely sighed, nodded and closed his eyes as my hands touched the sides of his face and broke his neck.

Frank sagged against me, death a welcome respite from the pain I might have otherwise caused. His unfastened pants were now down around his ankles, his bare bum exposed to the rest of the street. I tried very hard not to grab anything but saggy belly as I hauled him back towards his car.

I loved my exceptional strength. I leaned Frank against my shoulder and opened the rear door as quietly as possible, stuffing him inside like a plump sardine. All still seemed quiet in the neighbourhood, so I ducked around to the driver side door and slipped inside.

I started the car, the engine kicking back to life with a tiny roar and I drove off.

I was worried that I might encounter other Zone Security as we rolled away from my neighbourhood but possible discovery was a risk that I had to take. Consequences? Bring 'em on.

I didn't go very far at all. I slipped into one of the lonely streets several blocks from my own home, pulled up in the covered garage of an abandoned house and switched the engine off. I had no intention of staying for long. I'd eat my fill, then carry out the rest of my gruesome plan.

I climbed over the front seat and hopped in the back, sitting comfortably atop Frank's distended stomach as I grabbed one of his arms and pulled. The crunch of bone as I felt it disengaged from its socket, the horrific tearing of his flesh as I pulled the meaty limb from his body, still sickened me.

However, the smell and the oozing blood put an end to all thoughts of regret. I was chowing down on that arm like a chicken drumstick, tearing away unladylike portions of sinewy meat and swallowing them whole. The sticky saltiness of Frank's warm blood dribbled down my chin in its haste to escape my gluttonous hunger.

It took an hour and a half to eat the rest of Frank. I left his face and his fingers behind for identification, but I ate everything else. Well, except for his you-know-what.

I looked down. I was covered in blood and body bits. The backseat of the car looked like the aftermath of an exploding organic bomb.

Now to avoid making this murder look staged. I couldn't track blood back through to the front seat or Zone Security would suspect the vehicle had been moved after Frank's attack. I wanted the sweeper team to suspect that the occupants of the house I was planning on ditching the car in front of had done the deed.

So, I wiped my hands on the inside of my skirt and used a clean piece of fabric to open the door. I also left my shoes inside the car, so I could step out onto the driveway without leaving bloody footprints.

Moving quickly through the broken front fence and

into the backyard, I found a garden hose still attached to a rusting faucet. The water that gushed out was cold and brown, and smelt like wet rot. I'd washed in worse, though, and was hardly in a position to complain.

I hastily hosed myself from head to foot, standing naked in the darkness as I glistened.

I used the hair-tie wrapped around my wrist to pin back my dark hair before I headed back to the front of the house. I took my wet clothes with me, wringing them out and hefting them over my shoulder.

I waited for about ten minutes, shuffling from foot-to-foot in the darkness to help me dry off. It gave me plenty of time to reflect on my actions and debate whether to continue.

Evil me won.

After a few minutes, I slipped back into the front seat of the car and bundled my damp clothes into my lap. I fumbled for the ignition, the car finally kicking to life and my conscience finally waving little red flags as I popped the car into gear and backed out of the covered garage.

As I turned out on the open road again I immediately started to feel uneasy. I was completely exposed. Body parts were strewn across the backseat, and there was no way to possibly explain myself should I happen to be caught. My stomach rolled with every passing second, my fear of getting caught red-handed the only thing pressing my foot to the pedal and the pedal to the floor.

What had I done? What had this disease done to my humanity?

I made it without incident to Heather's house. Turning the headlights off, I parked Frank's car in her driveway and climbed out slowly, rolling up the windows to keep the smell inside. The last thing I wanted to do was attract the other zombies in the vicinity.

A last minute check saw me wiping down any surfaces I might have touched and grabbing my bloodied shoes off the floor in the backseat. My eyes lingered on the mess, raking the human debris for any evidence I might have left behind, and finding nothing. I took off towards the trees, my skin almost glowing and my body whole.

For the first time in weeks I felt truly free. Naked, I ran through the woods that backed onto Heather's house, the wind blowing against my flushed flesh as I carried away the blood-stained clothes from the murder I'd just committed.

Don't get me wrong—I wasn't proud of myself. I knew Frank was probably a good man, a man just trying to do his job, but he was still one of the reasons Nikki and most of the school had started to doubt me.

Guilt was a relative thing given my actions this night.

My exhilaration quickly faded. My jaunt through the woods had almost brought me clear across the Zone and a long way from home. Running naked through the streets may have sounded like a fun time if I'd have been Lady Godiva, but that had not been a part of my original plan. Then again, I hadn't really thought far past chowing down on Frank.

What the ...?

My heels skidded in the dirt and grass. I ducked behind a single tree lying at the edge of a small clearing and pressed my back against its roughhewn trunk. Shifting slowly around the peeling bark, I peered over my shoulder. In the distance I could see a figure fleeing as fast as a frightened deer, ducking and weaving through the last of the forest as it made a dash for suburban shrubbery.

A few more moments of stillness and the figure was on the move once more, barely avoiding the exposure of a bright street lamp as it darted down a side alley. The figure moved with the speed of the undead.

I stepped free of the tree's sheltering branches and followed. The smell of a fresh kill lay in the air and strengthened my suspicions. These zombies seemed to be everywhere, marking their territory and eating all of the goddamn food!

Reaching the last point of cover, I crept silently towards a rotting timber fence that separated the woods from suburbia beyond. The streetlight showed no mercy, its constant luminescence a barrier that would not stop me from confronting my foe.

I slipped around the fence, my nostrils flaring at the scent of blood coming from the leafy tips of the nearby shrubbery. I touched the sticky substance, rolled it between my fingers and sampled its saltiness across my tongue—wild boar-flavoured.

I glanced down the darkened alley. I was surprised to see that I had been wrong, that I was in fact standing in front of a long, cracked concrete driveway. A dimly-lit house lay at its end and a familiar car was parked near a rustic porch that lay at the front.

I paused. I was almost certain it was Connor's.

Realisation dawned. The fresh kill obviously belonged to Connor's aunt, a zombie just like me. Judging by the light now streaming through windows previously darkened, she was probably cleaning herself up and disposing of any evidence. That reminded me of the bloodied bundle of clothing and shoes still bunched against my chest.

'What the fuck …?'

Startled, I spun to find Connor standing right behind me. So much for my predatory senses. 'Shit!' I gasped, slapping his chest. 'You scared the crap out of me.'

Connor winced at my heavy touch and rubbed at his chest. 'What are you doing here, Palmer?'

'What am I doing? What the hell are *you* doing sneaking around in the middle of the night?'

He made no move to immediately answer. Eyes bulging, clearly Connor was a little distracted by the naked girl with a bloody bundle of clothing standing in his driveway. 'I was keeping an eye on my aunty.'

'Why?'

'I worry about her feeding habits. I just wanted to make sure it was an animal she was hunting and not a person, given how many of those are turning up dead lately.'

'Your aunt was hunting a boar, so she's off the hook.'

He nodded, eyes still focused on the clothes cinched tightly in my arms. 'Yeah, I know that she's doing the right thing.' He was quiet for a second, watching me as I fidgeted. 'Can I say the same thing about you?'

I looked away, knowing I couldn't answer him honestly.

'Here,' Connor said, holding his arms out for my clothes. 'My aunt always has a little fire going in the backyard in case she has to burn something in a hurry.'

I held them close, not sure I wanted to leave the evidence of my murder in someone else's hands. 'That's okay. I'll do it when I get home.'

'And, how are you going to get home?'

I shrugged. 'I'll run.'

Connor waggled impatient fingers at me, beckoning for me to pass him the clothes. I relented with a sigh, but followed him into the backyard, making sure that every last scrap of evidence was burned beyond recognition.

As my sneakers and favourite bra turned to cinders, the smell of blood was replaced with that of cedar-infused smoke. I turned away from the outdoor pizza oven, satisfied.

Connor was staring at me. I supposed I shouldn't have been surprised, being all naked. I wasn't sure whether I should dust my hands and congratulate him on a job well done or embrace him for some long overdue sex. 'Are you going to tell me why you're stalking my aunt?'

I scoffed, folding my arms across my bare chest. 'I didn't even know it was your aunt or your house until we crossed paths back in the woods. I was just running from my own crime scene, so to speak.'

'So you've fed.'

'Yes.'

'Can I ask why you needed to do it naked?'

I shrugged, looking down at my feet as I toed the grass. 'I made a bit of a mess.'

'Are you still hungry?' Connor asked, moving close enough that the warmth from the fire wasn't the only thing caressing my naked skin.

I quickly looked up as his fingers slowly skimmed the sides of my hips, his hands settling on the curve of my ribs. His thumbs lightly brushing the slight swell of my breasts. 'Um, yes.'

'You are?'

'Not for food,' I whispered. My arms snaked around his neck, secretly pleased that the rising desire that swelled and strained against the material of his jeans pressed for release.

Connor didn't offer to take me home right away. Instead, he took me down to the soft grass by the fire and spent the remaining hours of darkness continuously reminding me of what I had been missing.

I wondered how we didn't wake what was left of the neighbourhood, as each stroke of our hands elicited cries of pleasure. Why had I gone so long without killing? I'd been missing out on all the rewards of the flesh.

I worried that my rising hunger was becoming a reason to kill. Being in Connor's arms was making me question my own sanity. Were multiple orgasms worth more than the sanctity of human life?

It was a scary thought.

The answer? *Hell, yes!*

CHAPTER ELEVEN

Dear Diary,
Can't talk … too busy getting laid.

I slipped the diary behind my desk and turned around to crawl back into bed with Connor. It was still ridiculously early and the entire house was asleep, my boyfriend included. I supposed I'd worn him out again.

He'd taken me home soon after our quick rumble in the wild. We'd chased it with a quickie in the car, but then neither of us could bear to part with the other as we'd pulled up in our neighbour's driveway.

Bypassing that ridiculous excuse for a tent in the back-yard, I'd helped Connor climb up to my bedroom window, hauled his ass inside and then began to giggle wildly as he had a major freak out because a snake had followed us in.

Naturally, I caught the sucker and threw him in a box for safe-keeping. Sooner or later I'd be hungry again.

When Connor had calmed down and I'd gotten my laughter under control, we listened for sounds of movement within the house but all was quiet. Hungry kissing ensued, then yet another round of hard and fast sex. I really couldn't get enough of him.

As I slipped back under the crisp sheets that Mum had changed out the day before, Connor stirred in his sleep. He flung his arm out and caught me a sharp blow in the side of the head, then groaned and pulled me into him. He smelt like sex and sweat, a heady combination that had me curling into his side, my hands exploring southward.

He sniffed and rolled his head from side-to-side. Then he moaned a little, his eyes finally fluttered open. I didn't give him time to fully wake, my lips were already marking a moist trail between his neck and chest as he reached for me. My hips slid under the covers, my legs searching until I was straddling his pelvis.

'Hmm, good morning,' he murmured, springing to life beneath me. He squirmed, his hands holding me there, guiding me slowly onto him.

'It is now.' My eyes fluttered closed, pleasure over-taking coherent thought.

We spent the rest of those early hours locked in each other's arms, kissing without pause. He did his absolute best to maintain his stamina; I did my best not to scream and wake the household. We were equally successful on both accounts.

I shooed Connor out of the bedroom window just before seven. Mum would soon check on me and I was still supposed to be 'camping', so I followed him down the trellis work, this time making sure I was fully-dressed.

We kissed hastily, clumsily—like two idiots we grinned at each other—before he jumped the fence and headed for his car. I slipped inside the tent, only to find Jack curled up in my blanket and fast asleep against the pancakes Mum had the gall to call 'pillows'.

I smiled, creeping inside the fluorescent hole and laying down beside my baby brother. He had his slingshot tucked under one arm and the corner of the pillow in the other. When he felt the air mattress dip with my weight, his little eyes fluttered open, a big grin quickly spreading across his face.

'You got some food!' Jack chirped, sitting up slowly and rubbing at his sleepy eyes. 'You smell good, and your hair is pretty.'

'Thanks, buddy, but I have to ask: Why are you out here?'

He shrugged. 'I don't know. I miss you in the house, I guess.'

I struggled to look stern but he was being adorable. I *was* seriously concerned that he'd wandered down and slept in the backyard alone, though. 'You shouldn't have come out here alone. It's dangerous, Jack.'

He blew a raspberry at me, the full effect lost as he yawned and stretched. 'I have my slingshot.'

'That won't kill a hungry zombie, buddy.'

'I thought you would be here to protect me. Where'd you go, anyway?'

'I had to hunt.'

'Did you catch a great big bear with really sharp teeth?' Jack was quite excitable. He thought his sister could take on a bear and come home without a scratch or a drop of blood spilt on her clothes.

'Nah, I was hunting the two-legged variety of prey last night.'

Jack screwed his face up, not entirely certain what I'd just said, but he'd be smart enough to eventually figure it out.

'Come on, let's go inside and get you some breakfast,' I added, distracting him. 'You want what's left of those Coco Pops or do you want some toast?'

'Mum said we don't have any milk.'

'Probably because I keep eating all the cows.'

Jack liked that little joke, and cackled to himself all the way into the house.

'Where have you been?' Mum said, greeting me as I entered the kitchen behind Jack. She studied my appearance carefully, gave Jack the once-over and breathed a sigh of relief. 'You've fed,' she said, steadying herself against the edge of the dining table.

'Not on Jack.'

'I didn't say that.'

'But you were thinking it,' I chided, shaking a finger at her. A teasing smile crept across my face, and I found myself wrapping my arms around her waist and giving her a kiss on the cheek. 'Love you, Mum. Even if you did make me sleep in the backyard last night.'

'Which you didn't actually do!' she scoffed, unravelling my arms from around her and heading to the cupboard to get Jack his breakfast. She fished out a bowl, poured in some cereal and then slapped her forehead when she found there was no milk in the fridge.

'Katie ate all the cows,' Jack giggled, putting two pieces of bread into the toaster for himself.

The barest hint of a smile touched Mum's lips, before she slapped the counter and started to laugh. 'Oh, Katie, what are we going to do with you?'

'Hey, the white car that was parked across the street in the Fraser's driveway is gone,' Dad said, strolling into the kitchen. He went straight to the kettle and flipped the switch, pulling a mug and a tea bag out of the upper cupboard. He gave Mum a quick kiss on the cheek and stopped to pat the top of my head.

Dad paused, sniffed and then really saw me. 'You look better today.'

I nodded, now picking at my fingernails. 'Yeah, I had a good night out.'

'Should we ask?' Dad said, looking suddenly pale.

'Um, I probably wouldn't.'

Mum was no longer smiling. She still gripped at the edge of the kitchen bench, but now it was to support her weak knees. 'Anyone we know?'

Jack looked from me to Mum, knowing it was probably best not to intervene. Instead, he went back to studying the toaster with a zealous rapture, waiting for his bread to pop.

'It's probably best that you don't know the details.'

'Jesus Christ, Katie! Again?' Dad yelled, pulling at the confines of his tie and shoving a hand through his tousled hair.

'I'm a zombie, Dad, not a fucking vegan.'

Dad threw his arms into the air, and Mum slapped her hands over Jack's ears. 'Language,' she hissed, lowering her hands again.

'Yeah, Katie,' Jack grinned. 'Watch your *fucking* language.'

* * *

'Run, Katie, run!' Coach Salvatore yelled at me across the field. He held a stop watch in one hand and was waving at me excitedly with the other.

I liked Coach. He was a million times nicer than the last guy who'd trained the track team. That coach had grown overly-suspicious of my fluctuating aromas and had eventually confronted me. I gave him the usual denials, but the asshole still came at me with a javelin after practice.

Well, you know the story. Zombie Katie came back to life, ran after his pudgy ass, and then speared him to the car park median strip with his own javelin. I took my time eating him after that, relishing every, last suspicious morsel.

Our new coach was different, though, and seemed determined to see me succeed. He'd wanted me to enter the marathon, but since it had been cancelled he'd set his sights on loftier goals. What those were I simply didn't know yet, but it was good to have a hobby outside of picking the stringier parts of Frank out from between my teeth.

I picked up the pace, my legs moving faster than I ever thought possible. I was worried that the encouragement from Coach had me pushing forward with a little more inhuman speed than usual; if I had been, he showed no signs of being worried. Actually, just the opposite—he was jumping up and down, and cheering as I ran past the finish line.

'Katie,' he said, still waving his arms excitedly. 'You just ran ten kilometres in under twenty-five minutes!'

'I'm guessing that's a good thing,' I gasped, collapsing on the ground to catch my breath.

'Olympic qualifying times are about twenty-five to twenty-eight minutes.'

'Seriously?' I said, looking up at his excited face from the horizontal position. 'Bummer that no one runs the Olympics anymore, but Popmade stuffed that up for everyone.'

Coach Salvatore cleared his throat and put his hands on his hips. 'That may be so, but you have a lot of potential. The world will get back up on its feet again one day. It's just happening one little town at a time.'

I didn't bother to argue with him. The general population felt so safe and secure in the zoned areas but I knew of at least two zombies who hunted regularly in the area, and that didn't even include my stalker. 'Thanks for believing in me, Coach Salvatore. It's nice that someone does.'

Coach gently prodded my leg with his foot. 'Good to hear, now get to the showers and wash that sweat off. I'll see you tomorrow.'

I nodded my thanks and clambered quickly back to my feet. I was dying to know what had happened at Heather's house this morning when they'd found Frank's car in her driveway. Call me cruel, but that bitch had been making my life hell for well over a month and had it coming.

It was about time for some revenge.

I raced across the school oval and headed for the showers. I was in and out in record time, despite having to deodorise twice, shampoo twice and liberally applying anything that would obscure the smell.

I literally ran into Nikki in the corridor, her face momentarily lighting up as she recognised me. Then her expression shifted to one of wariness. 'Oh, hey!' she said, trying to instil some of her effervescent nature into those words.

'Hey, Nikki. I was just looking for you.'

'You were?' I realised how ominous my words had sounded and inwardly cursed. It wasn't like I was planning to gut her in the biology department and then roast her entrails in the boiler room below us.

'Yeah, didn't you want to go over some of the details for the winter formal this week? We've only got until Thursday.'

'Aw, shit, I forgot all about it,' Nikki said, slapping a hand to her forehead. 'I've been distracted this morning. Have you heard the news?'

'What news?'

And just like that she slipped right back into the wordy gossip I knew and loved. You could see how excited Nikki was, bouncing around on the balls of her feet and toes as her face lit up with untold drama. 'Okay, well, get ready for this.'

'I'm ready,' I said, joining in on the enthusiasm. I really just wanted to savour Heather's downfall, something I'd been planning since the start of semester.

'Well, after all the crap Heather's put you through over the last few weeks, it seems to have come back and bitten her in the ass.'

'What happened?'

'Wait for it—her entire family are under investigation.'

'No!' I gasped putting in my best Oscar-winning performance and relishing every minute of it. 'Give me the deets!'

Nikki took a second to calm herself, perhaps trying to decide on the appropriate amount of glee to show when discussing a person's imminent demise. 'Okay, so I heard that they found one of the Zone Security guys slaughtered in her driveway.'

'That doesn't mean she killed anyone or that any of her family killed anyone,' I said, trying to be circumspect. 'A zombie could have dragged the body there to eat it, or whatever.'

'But that's the thing,' Nikki whispered under her breath, a few students passing us by paying little heed. 'They didn't just find bits of the guy … he was found all over the backseat of the car and *that* was parked in the Rosenthal's driveway. Taylor said her dad thinks we might have another killer on our hands.'

I rolled my eyes. 'You have to stop listening to Taylor.'

'But her dad is Zone Security!'

I linked arms with Nikki and started to lead her towards the computer lab. I couldn't help but notice a few students who had recently shunned me now smiling shyly in my direction as I passed. I guessed it was hard to believe rumours coming from someone suspected of being the undead themselves. Maybe by winter formal on Friday night I'd be back to being plain old Katie Palmer again.

'Taylor's a gossip, just like Heather. Are you sure someone doesn't have their info mixed up?'

Nikki shook her head, hefting her backpack securely over one shoulder. 'Nah. Heather's next-door neighbour Toby saw the car for himself this morning. He said there was blood and guts everywhere.'

Not everywhere. I thought to myself, hiding a frown. *I'm not that much of a slob.*

'Oh well,' I said, and smiled brightly. 'I guess if Heather's innocent we'll know soon enough.'

'Don't sound so happy about it,' Nikki giggled, elbowing me in the side.

'Karma's a bitch and so is Heather. They should be the best of friends.'

Nikki chuckled a little more, resting her head briefly on my shoulder before she pushed the door to the computer lab open and yanked me in after her. 'I'm sorry I haven't been myself lately.'

'Don't stress on it,' I said, throwing my backpack onto the nearest bench. I swung a chair around and slumped back into the cushioning, stretching my long legs out in front of me. 'So what do we have left to plan for the winter formal?'

Nikki groaned, dropping into the chair beside me, her fingers already busying themselves with computer stuff just a little bit beyond my techtard know-how. 'Where do I even start?'

We huddled together for what felt like hours, trawling the Internet and trying to work out the logistics for the formal. We skipped out on two periods, and even ran into lunchtime to get everything organised before the weekend. The desk beside us was a mess of print-outs, photos and flyers.

Unfortunately, we knew our formal would never match the standards of the past. There were a lot of items now in short supply that used to be readily available, even simple things like streamers and balloons were no longer in production. We had to get creative or take what we could get. We'd also have to raise the funds for it ourselves.

Fucking zombies.

Nikki occasionally got chatty, curious about what could

have been happening with Heather and how it would affect the after-party. I didn't think one busty cheerleader would make the slightest difference to the outcome of the party. Students would still find alcohol somewhere and eventually converge on her uncle's cabin to celebrate, and at that point I suspected the noise and the lack of Zone Security in the immediate area would eventually see the night end in a bloodbath.

After all, that's why I was going.

When Nikki and I had finished up, she made a dash for the cafeteria before all the food was gone, and I headed back to my locker to prep for afternoon classes. To say that I was surprised to see Heather Rosenthal standing in front of my spray-painted, busted-up locker was an understatement.

'Hey, Heather,' I said, giving her a slight shove so I could get into my piece of crap locker. 'How's your day been?'

'How's my day been?' she rasped, spittle flying from her thin-lipped mouth.

'I'm guessing not well?'

'And you fucking know it!' she screamed, slamming a fist against my locker and jamming my hand inside.

'Ahh, shit,' I gasped, pulling out my hand and shaking it, the books clattering to the floor all but forgotten. 'Was that necessary?'

'You dumped a dead body in my driveway, so you tell me?'

I studied my hand and the torn skin across the knuckles. I didn't hesitate to lick the blood off, knowing it was dangerous for anyone near me to be exposed. 'Really, Heather? You're blaming me for the bloody buffet in your front yard?'

Heather's face puckered inwards like she'd been sucking on a basket of lemons, as she watched me delight in the taste of my own flesh and blood.

'I mean, seriously,' I continued, taking long, languorous licks of blood while eyeballing her, 'do you really think I sat in the backseat of that car and took my time picking the flesh off the body, sucking the marrow from his bones and drinking the juices from his eyeballs while you slept soundly inside?'

I derived serious pleasure from watching her eyes widen, her previously pursed lips now forming a silent O. All colour had dripped from the folds of her face. She started to mouth noiseless words but her breath appeared trapped, emitting tiny rasping sounds in her effort to speak.

I cocked my head to the side. 'Sorry? I can't hear you, Heather,' I teased, leaning closer to her trembling form.

'I-I ...'

'You, you?'

'I n-never said anything about t-the b-b-backseat.'

'Didn't you?' I pressed, taking another step towards her. Heather backed into the locker behind her, her hands splaying against the cold metal surface. No escape.

'No.'

'Hmm. I wonder what that means?'

'You d-did it, d-didn't you?' Heather whispered. Her tongue darted out to moisten her drying lips.

I checked over my shoulder. The corridor was still blissfully clear of observers—the sound of boisterous cheers, laughter and general chatter were mostly coming from the direction of the cafeteria.

When I looked back at Heather she was still shaking like a Chihuahua dumped in a toilet bowl. She flinched as I invaded the last remnants of her personal space, placing a hand on the lockers either side of her head. 'Well, you'll never hear me openly admit to something so conniving, terrifying and utterly despicable but if I were you, I'd consider the body parts in your driveway as a warning.'

'A warning?' she murmured, swallowing.

I nodded and then slowly looked her up and down. I took

my time, making sure her skin crawled from all those horror-filled thoughts in her head. 'Sure. I mean, the flesh-eater in question polished that meal off in record time. Imagine what they could do to a tiny piece of blonde fluff like you.'

I snapped my teeth. Heather flinched, banging her head violently against the locker behind her.

'I get it,' she said hastily. 'Honestly, Katie, I won't say anything.'

I pushed away from the lockers, putting plenty of space between us. 'I'm glad to hear you say that, Heather. I was starting to think that maybe you didn't like me, what with all the bitchiness and accusations pointed in my direction.'

Heather laughed nervously, sliding closer and closer towards freedom. Her fingers soon found the corner of the wall and propelled her forward into the empty corridor, which would soon be filled with a throng of bored teens making their way to afternoon classes. 'I'm going to go now.'

I shrugged, barely able to contain my mirth. 'I'll see you at the winter formal.'

Heather didn't answer, just spun on her heels and took off down the corridor like she was being chased by the Grim Reaper himself. I waved.

Mission accomplished.

The echo of her hurried footsteps as they slapped down the corridor was very satisfying. Who would have thought that a Monday morning at school could be so enjoyable?

I checked my conscience, waiting for that pang of guilt at Heather's misery or the incessant pull of do-gooding that would extinguish my good mood. My heart seemed light though, absent of such a filter. All I could think of was the ever-pressing weight of concern that was hammering my family because of people like Heather.

Oh well—such is unlife.

CHAPTER TWELVE

Dear Diary,

Well, school's back to normal now. People have stopped staring at me like I can strip the flesh from their body with just a look and Heather's being a decent human being—well, at least she's stopped the taunting and no longer encourages others to partake.

Speaking of Heather, she was acquitted of all formal charges, as I knew she would be. I can't say the same for her dad. ~~Turns out he's just like me, though obviously much more discreet about his second life ... at least, he was until I dumped a body in the driveway.~~

I feel a little bad about that.

Winter formal is set for tonight but no one really cares. It's the after-party that everyone's raving about, though Heather seems less enthused than before. I guess finding out your dad's a zombie will do that to you.

On a side note, I gotta admit I'm a little freaked out at the moment. I've been sneaking out most nights ~~to hunt~~ *but I have the feeling I'm being followed again. I can't do anything without looking over my shoulder. At first I thought Heather might still be following me, but I realised that whoever it is can clearly keep up with me.* ~~So, not a human, then.~~

I've been thinking about Mrs Cook a lot lately. Her words of warning keep playing over and over in my head. I've been trying to figure who might have a grudge against me, but—

dropped the pen on my desk. The ink-filled cylinder rolled across the uneven surface until it teetered on the edge and finally fell, hitting the floor with a forgettable *thud*.

I stumbled to my feet and kicked my chair back, unconcerned as it fell to the floor with a more pronounced crash than the discarded pen. I was already racing to the window, parting the heavy drapery in an effort to catch a second glimpse of what I thought I'd just seen.

Had I been human I might not have seen the hurried blur of colour registered by my predatory eyes—a flash of long hair and a slip of milky-white skin. Greater detail was hopefully soon to follow, but I knew enough to say that I'd just seen a female zombie loitering in *my* backyard.

With my face pressed against the cool glass, I studied the perimeter carefully, taking my time to scan every possible hiding place.

Seeing nothing, I gripped the window pane and slid it open, ducking my head out into the fresh night air to bring my other senses to bear. There it was, that same jasmine and vanilla perfume that had lingered in the air by Mrs Cook the morning I'd gone running. It remorselessly tickled at my nose, begging for me to seek out its owner and bring them to justice.

Justice, however, was a word for those with a conscience; I could no more judge this zombie for eating humans then I could myself. But, why was I still being followed by this over-zealous flesh-eater? Was she playing a game? If so, why was I the focus?

She had not harmed me physically or left trophies on my doorstep to out me like I had outed Heather. She'd made no attempt to make contact, mark her territory, or leak snapshots of me devouring my victims to the Zone Authority.

So why all the hiding in shadows and watching me? What was I missing?

I caught a brief glimpse of her shiny hair, flowing like an auburn mane as it disappeared over the back of the fence. I got an eyeful of crimson silk that snagged and tore off on a stubborn paling.

I launched into action.

Taking my time while I climbed down the trellis work and avoided destroying what was left of Mum's little garden wasn't an option. In one swift movement, I vaulted from the window and plummeted to the earth. Landing with a *thud*, I cursed like a drunken sailor. I brushed the dirt from my knees and then climbed unsteadily back to my feet.

There was no time to waste. I'd twisted my ankle, but I pushed the pain back into a compartment in the deep recesses of my mind, ignoring it as I headed for the fence.

Gripping the wood, I quickly swung myself over, swearing once more as I landed on my swollen limb. Yep, I'd need to eat some fresh meat soon if I wanted this injury to fully heal.

'Get out my yard!' our neighbour shouted, bravely emerging from a garden shed in the corner. His fist was shaking above his bald head with unvoiced accusation. The other zombie had obviously been faster than me; it had already cleared the front fence and headed for the street.

'Sorry, Mr Bobi-nacker-nackle,' I shouted, dusting myself off again and making for the front fence. 'I was just leaving.'

'It's Bobber-nackering!' he shouted after me, annoyed because I'd been calling him 'Bobi-something-whatever' since I was kid. I'd never really cared enough to remember his actual name, but I supposed I should have cared now.

Mr Bobi-neutering seemed to agree because he lunged for his garden hose and fired it up. I spent the rest of my run to the front fence dodging a glacial stream of high-pressured water and failing miserably. I was pegged to the fence about four times before I managed to dive around the side of his house and out of range.

Exhausted, I scrambled over the fence as yet another jet of water slammed into my back, but was buffeted back by the palings. I was drenched, but on the move again, my pumping footsteps slapping like wet fish against the pavement.

A car engine—sounding close, but just out of sight— roared to life like an angry lion ruling over his pride. I heard gears crunch and tyres squeal as they spun on the asphalt, trying to find traction.

I rounded the corner only a second before the car peeled away from the curb and took off down the street. I was too far away to make out much detail in the darkness of night, and the driver had been smart enough to park underneath a busted streetlamp. I only got a partial on the rear left bumper and the licence plate. The car was silver, but so were a million others parked in driveways or abandoned in the streets all over my Zone.

By the time I had any chance of identifying who it was, the car had already screeched around a nearby corner and disappeared out of sight.

'Stupid fucking kids!' a neighbour yelled out their front window. I didn't know the guy, but I bet he lobbied the Zone Authority for more sterilisation and more speed bumps in his spare time.

Still, his expletive was telling—had the neighbour just seen an out of control car with an out of control teen at the helm? Did that mean I needed to be searching closer to home? Was it possible that I lived near or went to school with someone just like me—a zombie?

That was food for thought, not that I had much time to

mull it over. I was supposed to be getting ready for the winter formal; instead, I'd been jumping fences like a naughty show-horse and had been hosed down for my trouble.

I sighed, hands clasped on top of my head as I stared after the vanished car. There was no point dwelling on it. Connor was coming to pick me up in an hour, and I was standing in the middle of the street after dark—yet another infringement of Zone regulations. I was staring to make a habit of that.

* * *

'Have I told you how beautiful you look tonight?' Connor whispered the words in my ear as he led me through school security and into the corridors.

'Must have been the top-up rat I snacked on beforehand,' I joked, thankful for the mousetraps Dad had setup in the roof. My ankle no longer hurt, and my dark hair looked particularly shiny tonight as it skimmed down the length of my spine.

Connor nipped at my neck, his lips quivering with soft laughter. 'For future reference, talking about your vermin diet is not a turn-on.'

'Oh, please.' I gave him a little shove and sent him flying into the lockers beside us. 'If I took my dress off right now you wouldn't give a shit about what I'd just said.' I helped Connor steady himself, shooting him an apologetic look.

He slinked an arm around my waist again, his fingers playing with the silken threads at my hips. 'You're probably right. Shall we find out?'

I smirked, turning so I could plant a chaste kiss on the side of his cheek. 'Let's just enjoy the night and see what happens.'

'So that's a "yes" to corridor sex?'

'Shut up, Connor.'

The sound of pumping music blaring through the open doors of the gymnasium drowned out Connor's retort. As we stepped inside, I found myself rather pleased with the result. All the hard work Nikki had put into the decorating had paid off.

Paper cups taken from the cafeteria had been individually painted and hung from coloured string at various angles across the room. Inside were tiny tea lights—ambient, but definitely a fire hazard. As the night progressed, the addled seniors would start dipping further into their secret stashes of alcohol and attempt to slam-dunk the paper cups into the bleachers, just like they always did.

Nikki had also managed to convince the school band to play. They weren't very good but options were a little light these days, and at least they had the instruments the right way around. Their music erred on the side of classical, but occasionally someone hit a drum or stroked a guitar.

It definitely wasn't the winter formal we'd imagined, but it was nice to be able to still celebrate something after all the attacks and recent deaths. The world wasn't the same and accepting that fact was crucial. We couldn't pretend that the factories would re-open any time soon and that all the products we'd taken for granted in the past would magically reappear on supermarket shelves. That was a pleasant dream but an unrealistic one.

And I had no idea what I was going to do when I ran out of concealer.

'Palmer? You okay?'

I shook my head. I hadn't realised that Connor had been trying to talk to me. He studied me with concern, his brow wrinkled. 'Sorry. Just daydreaming, I guess.'

I was yet to tell Connor about my antics earlier in the

evening. I hadn't told him about any of the incidents yet. Despite his acceptance of what I was, I didn't think he really wanted to know what I did in the late hours of the night, unless it included giving him a—

'Look, there's Heather,' Connor muttered, pointing to the twitching blonde in the corner. She was all alone, hands nervously clasped in front of her and her bottom lip trembling. 'She looks miserable.'

'Heather just found out her dad's a zombie.'

'No shit?' Connor said, dragging me out onto the dance floor. He wound his arms around my waist, suddenly possessive, and pulled me close. My hands began to inch up his arms until they encircled his neck. We swayed with the beat, and I soon forgot all about Heather. Connor still appeared distracted, though.

'What's wrong?'

He hesitated before answering. 'Look, don't get me wrong. I think the way Heather's been treating you recently is shit, but I kinda feel bad for her now. I mean, I know what it's like having someone close to you turn.'

'You're talking about your aunt.'

He nodded, moving us deeper into the throng of languid dancers. I tried to concentrate on his movements, the feel of his body against mine.

Connor's feet stopped shuffling, an abrupt halt that saw me collide heavily with his chest. He strained upwards, his eyes searching the crowd. 'Whoa.'

'What's wrong now?' I said, standing on my tippy toes to see what all the fuss was about. 'Is Heather imploding?'

'No,' Connor muttered, dropping his arms from my hips. 'I'll be right back.'

'Wait, where are you going?'

'To deal with my aunt.'

'She's here?'

Connor didn't answer. He was already winding his way through the crowd, quickly blending into the scents and sounds of everyone around us. I tried to keep up with him, supremely curious to meet the woman who had murdered his entire family and yet still managed to earn back his love and trust, but Connor moved like water in a river bed, flowing quickly and rushing away.

'Katie!'

I spun on my heels, turned mostly by the hand that had grabbed my shoulder. Nikki was standing behind me, dressed in a form-fitting emerald green dress. Her curly red hair was pulled back into a tight bun, the fallen tendrils framing her delicate features. Her makeup was perfect, and the smile she wore was so wide and triumphant that I couldn't help but beam back at her. 'Hey, Nikki. You did a great job with the formal.'

'Thanks to you,' she gushed, rushing in for a breath-stealing squeeze. She stepped back again, reaching down and gripping my hands tightly in hers. 'I'm so glad that you came, even after everything you've been through and the way people have been treating you.'

I shrugged, knowing that the only reason the limelight had found another victim was because I'd focused it elsewhere. Heather Rosenthal now stood in my shoes, weaker and more unprepared for the title of pariah than I had been. The first pangs of guilt over my actions finally started to dig their accusatory fingers into my conscience.

I shook off that negativity and straightened my long, flowing dress around me. Then I smoothed my hair from my face, puckered my lips to refresh the lipstick, and gave Nikki another quick hug. 'Can I catch up with you later for a longer chat? I've just got something I need to do.'

Nikki was taken aback by my abruptness and the whiplash change in conversation, but only slightly, as a microsecond later her smile was back. 'Sure, I guess. I probably should go and make sure that Justin isn't spiking the punch, anyway.'

I pointed to a couple of the inebriated football jocks brushing up on their routine. One was dry humping the empty space in front of him while his mates cheered on, the other whipping an imaginary ass. 'I think you might have missed the boat on that one, Nikki. People are already in after-party mode.'

'But the formal only started an hour ago!' she moaned, practically stamping her feet. Soon she forgot about me and began to trample people on her way to the punch bowl. She bent to sniff its contents, and then turned and looked back at me, a disgusted expression on her face.

I was cackling, knowing that all attempts to cram common sense down a teenager's throat were a complete waste of time, unless it came perfectly packaged in a bottle of Jim Beam or a pack of cheap-ass Vodka Coolers.

Leaving Nikki to the football team, I turned back to look for Connor but he was still nowhere in sight. I made it my mission to find him. Dancing on my own just made me look like a try-hard—I always defaulted to moves too reminiscent of *Saturday Night Fever*.

I ignored the football jock who was still slapping that imaginary ass as I walked on by and headed for the door. I stopped at the opening, stepping up onto the seats of the bleachers to get an elevated view of the room. I still couldn't see Connor, but I could see Heather. She'd found a few of the cheerleaders from her squad to mingle with. She wasn't overly-emotive or vocal but at least she looked more comfortable, which was more than I could say for Trenton Debrovnic. He'd sandwiched himself into the corner as if he were invisible, watching others dance while his foot kept beat.

Oh, God. Why am I worried about the school nerd right now?

Leaving Trenton to his one-man boogie, I ditched the formal and headed into the school corridors to hunt for Connor and his aunt. Zone Security held me up at the door. I was unescorted and without transport—a security breach.

'My date came through here,' I tried to explain, making another effort to exit the building but to no avail.

'Are you referring to the blonde guy with his mum?'

'Aunty, but whatever. Can someone please take me to them?'

The gruff security man with his tidy uniform, crisp hat and shiny black boots shook his head at me. 'No can do. Unless you have someone waiting to pick you up or ready to escort you to your vehicle, we've been instructed to keep the students inside where it's safe.'

I rolled my eyes and walked over to stand by one of the wide, bay windows instead. Connor would pass back through here eventually and maybe, just maybe I'd catch a glimpse of them in the car park beforehand.

As luck would have it, that's exactly what happened. I glimpsed the back of Connor's sandy blonde hair, his crisp black, dinner jacket, and the arm he had slung around a slender woman's tall shoulders. She had auburn hair that she'd swept high into a soft bun and had poured herself into a figure-hugging mini-dress that hardly seemed age appropriate.

I couldn't see either of their faces—the distance was too great and they were facing away from me, presumably heading to whatever vehicle she came in. From the rear the two looked nothing alike, but how do you compare shoulders, waists and backsides?

What the—

I was rooted to the spot, my nose pressed against the glass like a panther in the zoo. The coincidence seeming impossible, but the car Connor's aunty was getting into looked like the very same car I'd seen peeling away from that street curb earlier tonight? It had a silver body, a dented rear bumper and with the partial on the plate it definitely matched.

I believe I'd just found my zombie.

Why the fuck was Connor's aunty following me?

CHAPTER THIRTEEN

I sat pressed against the glass, waiting for what felt like hours for Connor to return. I stared at the glowing tail-lights of his aunt's car as it moved slowly through the gravel strewn car park and finally faded into the night.

I could feel my fingers curling into fists at my sides—not out of anger, but to keep myself grounded. My nails dug painfully into the softness of my palms, the crescent indentations reminding me to keep still and to keep calm. I didn't want to rush off looking for answers.

Hopefully, Connor hadn't been holding out on me.

I kicked the concrete wall as I watched Connor stare after the departing vehicle, and then finally make his way back towards the school's entrance. He had his hands buried in his pockets and eyes to the ground, though he kept glancing back over his shoulder. Perhaps he was trying to reassure himself that his aunt had definitely left.

As Connor reached the entrance, he was held up briefly by security. Despite having watched him leave only minutes before, they still felt the need to interrogate him upon his return.

I moved in, my floral dress billowing around me as I approached. Connor's lips lifted when he saw me, and some of the tension eased from his shoulders. 'He's with me.' I motioned, hooking my right arm through his left one and dragging him down the corridor.

There were a few verbal protests as we hurried off, but they were just words. Clearly the rent-a-cops were bored with their Friday night posting and wanted to flaunt some of their meagre powers. I supposed they could have been acting super-cautious because an eviscerated Frank had turned up but more likely just hated having to babysit us teens.

'We need to talk,' I said to Connor, ushering him past the gym doors and towards one of the locked classrooms. On the dance floor I could see some of the braver students wildly gesticulating, their dance moves unfounded, while the drunks were making it their mission to lock lips with any other willing participants. There weren't many.

With bigger fish to fry, I instead headed for the computer lab. I yanked the door hard enough to bust the locking mechanism, and with creaking hinges, it swung open.

'Palmer, is something wrong?' Connor asked, attempting to close the door behind us. It caught in the frame and slowly started to creak open again.

'Leave it,' I muttered, and jumped up onto the edge of the teacher's desk. 'I need to talk to you about your aunt.'

'My aunt? Why?'

I took a steadying breath, still not sure how to broach the topic. 'She's been following me, Connor.'

He shook his head in disbelief, folding his muscular arms across his chest and digging his fingers into the warm pockets under his arms. He paced, a thousand thoughts undoubtedly ploughing through his mind, thoughts that I wished I could reach in and grab. Something wasn't right here.

'Connor, you need to talk to me.'

His beautiful blue eyes met mine as he walked back across the room. Connor looked annoyed, confused—so many emotions were crossing his face that I couldn't keep up.

He moved towards me now, leaned silently against the rolled edge of the old desk and crossed one of his long legs over the other. He unfolded his arms, his eyes cast to the ground. Lips pursed and then flattened, and then the lower one was suddenly lost to the inner sanctum of his mouth.

'Connor …' I pressed, determined to get an answer. 'Tell me what you're thinking. You look like you know something.'

'No,' he said, shaking his head again. 'I just don't understand.'

'Someone has been following me around for a couple of months,' I muttered. 'I had no idea who until tonight.'

'This is the first time you've mentioned it to me.'

'It's the first time I've mentioned it to anyone,' I corrected, leaning forward to clasp my hands across the top of my thighs. 'I haven't ever felt threatened, not really, so I didn't press the issue. I mean, I've wondered and asked myself a million questions, but it wasn't until Mrs Cook died that I started to take it a little more seriously.'

'What does Mrs Cook have to do with anything?' Connor asked, his eyes leaving the solace of the floor to search my face.

'I'm the one that found her,' I admitted. 'She was dying but still tried to warn me that someone—a female zombie—was after me.'

Connor scoffed. 'And you think it's my aunt? No offence, but why the hell would she care about you?'

I shrugged, my fingers knotting together like pretzels in my lap. 'I don't know. Like I said, I've never actually felt threatened, just that someone was watching. Mrs Cook was as high as a kite from all the pain and could have been talking crap due to blood loss. I mean, she said some stuff to me but …' I shook my head, dispelling the uncertainty.

195

'Despite what I may or may not understand yet, that doesn't change the fact that your aunt and I had a little encounter tonight. I want to know why.'

'Are you sure it was her?' Connor asked, twisting around to rest a leg up on the desk. We stared at each other across the small divide. His brow was creased. A small part of me suspected that he thought I was talking rubbish.

I cringed and carefully contemplated my next answer. Connor badly wanted to believe that his aunt, the former biter, was totally reformed, and perhaps she was. Why then would she have followed us to the formal tonight? The woman seemed to have an agenda, and neither Connor nor I knew what it was.

'I saw her through my bedroom window tonight. I didn't know it was your aunt at the time, and I didn't see her face, but I did see her drive away.'

'Are you absolutely certain?'

I reached out to smooth my fingers over the top of his, waiting for him to soften and take my hand. He didn't. I eventually gave up and tucked my hands back in my lap. 'The car from earlier tonight was the same car she got into a few minutes ago.'

Connor pinched the bridge of his nose, squeezing tightly enough that when he pulled away the flesh was red. 'Why would she be following you?'

'Your guess is as good as mine. Why did she come here tonight?'

'She didn't really say.'

'Come on,' I urged. 'Why did you send her away then?'

'Isn't it obvious? She's a zombie, Palmer. She's been able to keep her hunger under control, but only just. The last thing I wanted to do was put her in a room with some sweaty, stupid teens just begging to be her next meal.'

I frowned. 'Are you kidding me? You *do* remember who you're speaking to, right?'

'It's different with you. You keep yourself under complete control.'

'That's ridiculous. Do you even know how hard it is to be with you sometimes, how hard it is for me to go to school here?'

'I hear you, Palmer,' Connor argued, 'but my aunt has fed on a lot of human flesh. She has trouble keeping to the straight and narrow now. She argues with me constantly, telling me that animals don't satisfy her hunger anymore. That's why I follow her—to make sure she doesn't kill anyone.'

'Then, why would she be following me?'

'I don't know.'

He seemed sincere, but it was obvious to me that Aunty Z snuck away quite a lot when Connor wasn't looking.

My head whipped to the side. I'd just heard the sound of scuffling and a muffled scream from the corridor. Connor mirrored my movement, and together we both strained to hear the commotion outside.

Connor beat me to the computer lab door because my dress had caught on the edge of the desk as I'd launched myself forward. A small hole resulted from that hasty action, but I couldn't care less. The smell of blood was so thick, so tangible, in the air that it almost sent me to my knees.

'What is it?' he asked, holding my hand to prevent me stumbling further. The sound of gunshots answered, and a look of fear twisted Connor's features. It slipped like a knife of dread into the pit of my stomach.

We rushed through the doorway and out into the corridor. People were pouring through the gym door, pushing and shoving with no thought to the welfare of those around them. Screaming, a sound like music, accompanied the incessant pounding of footfalls across the shiny corridor floor.

The sickening thud of bodies as they fell, trapped under stampeding feet, was second only to the slipping of shoes on the sticky crimson substance that coated the floor.

Connor and I ran towards the gym and chanced a look through the double doors—bloodied faces with beaming white teeth could be seen inside, tearing chunks away from live human flesh. I had no idea how so many zombies had managed to get inside the school grounds or where Zone Security was, but I could see that my classmates were seriously fucked.

I counted three hungry outsiders and two other of my fellow students that had apparently been doing a better job than me at keeping their infection a secret. Dropping the charade and bringing out their knives and forks as they'd been overwhelmed by the flesh feast, these few were unable to stop themselves from partaking in what was now freely on offer.

'Holy shit,' Connor gasped, trying to tug me in the opposite direction. 'We have to get out of here!'

'No shit, Sherlock.'

I wasn't scared to be amongst my own kind—even the fleshier, more desperate ones—but I was afraid to linger. If I stayed much longer, I might be tempted to feast on the carcasses strewn across the gymnasium floor myself. They were sparkling with the paper confetti Nikki had spent hours punching out by hand and looked like dinner specials, their insides spilling out as the eager zombies voraciously ripped them open.

I'd already taken a few steps towards freedom, fuelled by Connor's desperate pleas to leave the building, when a slither of auburn hair caught my attention. Initially, I thought it was just blood-streaked, but then I recognised the French knot and freckly shoulders to which the hairdo belonged. 'Connor, wait.'

'Hell, no!' He shouted, his voice wavering. He attempted to pull me towards the exit again, but it was a pointless exercise.

'Connor, I think I can see your aunt.'

'Can't be,' he shouted again, trying to raise his voice over the screaming. The sounds seemed to mingle together perfectly, a symphony of death.

I craned my neck to see clearly, but my vision was impaired by the bodies still filing out of the room. Strangely, some of the zombies were merely catching, biting and releasing them—a sure-fire way to create more of us, but to what end?

I let go of Connor's hand. There was no point trying to fight him on this. He could still be hurt, so letting him go was the right thing to do. I slipped through a small gap in the throng of fleeing teens, putting some distance between us. As I moved, I caught sight of Nikki's tear-stained face, relieved to see that she appeared unharmed.

Then she was screaming as one of the zombies grabbed her ankle, yanking hard enough to pull her down to her knees. My conscience debated for a millisecond—pursue Connor's aunt or help my best friend avoid zombification?

I dove to help Nikki. I hissed, surprised to find myself baring my teeth at Trenton, the nerdy computer tech. I hadn't picked that one. He'd always seemed weak-willed and easily dominated by the school social hierarchy. Luckily, he was just as easily scared off as a zombie.

Trenton rolled away, off to stalk another unsuspecting victim. Blood covered his face and hands, his stomach distended from feeding. I knew that compulsion well, the need to keep taking your fill until there was nothing left of the body but bones.

'Katie!' Nikki screamed, her voice hoarse.

I wrapped my arms around her and helped her to her feet. She was shaking uncontrollably, sobbing against my shoulder. 'W-what the hell's happening?'

'I don't know,' I said, trying to soothe her. 'I guess there were more teen zombies in our school than we thought.'

'*These things are supposed to be our friends!*'

'Not anymore,' I mused, trying to keep her steady despite her shaking knees. 'You have to get out of here, okay?'

'Not without you,' she cried, gripping me almost painfully by the arm.

'There's someone else in here that I need to find.'

'*Fuck them!*' Nikki shouted, trying to haul me back towards the door. It appeared adrenalin had endowed her with something approaching super-human strength. 'These people are trying to eat us, Katie. We need to get out of this school now!'

We were separated a second later by another mass of panicked classmates heading for the door. I could see that most of them were bitten and bled from gaping wounds on their arms, legs and shoulders. Some were not going to make it through the night. The ones that did …

Nikki was screaming again, but this time she'd been pushed in the right direction. Her body was sandwiched between those trying to escape and the doorframe, which was pressing viciously into her back. She held her hands out to me, straining with every bit of her body to reach me, but eventually slipped away.

Nikki would be safe for now.

I focused back on the room, my stomach rolling with painful waves of desire. I imagined my hands were slick with that crimson life-force, my face buried in innards. The room smelt like death and frenzied excitement, and I wanted to be a part of it, but knew that any blood on my lips would be my undoing.

I couldn't see Connor anywhere. I was praying he had made it out safely, had run into Nikki in the corridors and helped her get outside. The sounds of gunshots nearby still worried me. I prayed that Zone Security weren't shooting first and asking questions later.

There! A flash of ghostly skin and an unravelling twist of auburn hair peeked out through the bloodied crowd. Long, limber legs darted across the room, pulling me deeper into the advancing mass. I could see that most of the senior class had now emptied into the corridors, and the feeding group had begun to thin out.

Only stragglers and victims were left.

I moved quickly, kicking Trenton in the ass as I passed. He was now buried neck-deep in one of the fallen cheerleaders. That was probably a dream come true for the computer nerd.

I kept my eyes trained on the prize. Across the dance floor, I could see Connor's aunt now bobbing from side-to-side as she teased her next victim.

There was a strangled scream and then the bobbing and weaving stopped in favour of more brazen tactics. Connor's aunt moved in, wrapping her hand around what I realised was my archenemy's throat. I could see Heather over the redhead's shoulder, squirming in her grip, eyes wide and lips parted as she gasped for air.

Once again, I was at a crossroads.

On one side, my mind's eye could see the land of Retribution, a gravel-lined road marked with more red flags than a bullfighting competition. A new billboard marked the landscape in the distance. Smoothed across the front was a picture of me wearing a cap backwards and a pair of eighties parachute pants, busting a move on a checkerboard dance floor. Heather was there, of course, rapping with her last gasping breath, her waning pulse the beat my feet were happily hammering out on the hardwood. The slogan at the bottom read, 'Guilt is for pussies'.

I glanced in the other direction. Small flowers marked the tree-lined, cobblestone street that led off into the distance. Just like in *Song of the South*, birds chirped in the branches and old Uncle Remus was singing 'Zip-a-Dee-Doo-Dah' at me from the sidelines.

The billboard on this side was marked by a wreath of red poppies, and the picture here showed me dressed up in a nun's habit. There was a look of bliss on my face as my eyes searched heavenward for solace, a small halo ringing the top of my head. Heather was writhing around on the ground and kissing my zombie-pocked feet. I was already frowning at the slogan: 'Saving the world, one bitch at a time'.

Should I breakdance or should I be merciful?

Decisions, decisions.

A sigh escaped my lips, which very quickly became a groan as I lunged forward, my feet propelling me across the gym floor.

I wasn't fast enough. Before I could reach them, Connor's aunt yanked Heather close to her and sank her teeth into the fleshy spot at the top of Heather's shoulder.

Blood poured from the open wound like a ruby fountain, spilling down the front of Heather's sequined dress and pooling on the floor. She would have screamed if she hadn't been gasping for breath.

A second later I was barrelling into the aunt, sending her and Heather to the hardwood floor like two sacks of potatoes. Heather scrambled away as quickly as her legs would take her, clawing at her throat for breath and then crying out.

'Katie!' a familiar voice shouted at me, just as I was bringing my fist back to punch Connor's aunt in the temple.

I stopped just before the point of impact, my fist a mere millimetre from doing permanent damage. I sat there straddling her, the sound of that voice filling my thoughts with calm. If I was honest with myself, her voice always had.

'Dr Chalmers?' I whispered, moving closer. I inspected her face, making sure that it really was her under the mussed hair, and bloodied nose, lips and chin. I'd only seen Connor's aunt from behind before now.

'Yes, Katie, it's me.'

'You're Connor's aunt?'

She nodded as best as she could from her place on the floor.

'What are you doing here?'

'I'm trying to protect Connor.'

'By eating the pep squad?' My voice was high and barely recognisable.

'You don't understand,' she reasoned, trying to edge her way out from underneath me. I held firm, squeezing my thighs around her midsection. 'Connor is all I have left.'

'Yeah, but only because you ate everyone else.'

She gave me that stern frown, her dark eyes becoming angry slits. 'I cannot deny that I struggled during the initial outbreak, but it was never my intention to hurt my family. That's why I've found working with you so fascinating, Katie. You are the first one of us that I've met that seems to be able to reason her way through the bloodlust.'

'You think?'

Dr Chalmers attempted to nod again. 'Definitely. Even

after I left a trap for you and offered you up someone you knew, you still refused to eat them, despite your hunger.'

'Holy shit! You're the one who killed Mrs Cook.'

Heather moaned behind us, quickly pressing a hand to cover her mouth. I turned to glare at her.

'I need to feed to stay fresh,' Dr Chalmers continued. 'I took your teacher to the marathon track where I knew you'd be training. I fed from her but left her alive, and apparently, so did you.'

I shook my head, trying to digest her words. 'But how did her body end up clear across town?'

'I couldn't have you suspected of murder, Katie. You mean too much to my nephew. I wanted to test you, but I didn't want to see you get caught, either.'

'And that's why the video store guy in Zone Three was found with the body.'

'Yes.'

I slowly slid off Dr Chalmers and crawled closer to Heather, who whimpered and curled herself into a ball. The doctor sat up slowly, smoothing out her mini-dress and making a conscious effort to straighten her hair.

'So, what now?' I asked, watching her eyes dart backwards and forwards between the frightened girl at my back and myself.

'Now I finish her and then we go home.'

'You can't eat Heather,' I objected. 'She may deserve it, but you've already condemned her enough by biting her.'

'Nothing short of what she deserves for the way she's been treating you.'

I raised an eyebrow, concerned that my heated discussions in therapy had been taken way out of context. Sure, I wasn't a fan of Heather—I probably never would be—but that didn't mean that I wanted to see her in my therapist's mouth and all over the gym floor.

'Connor has told me all about what you've had to endure lately,' Dr Chalmers continued, creeping closer. 'I think he may have some very deep feelings for you, Katie, and knowing that made me want to protect you. I wanted to erase anyone who may have gotten in the way of your combined happiness.'

I considered that prospect. 'Fine. You can eat her lips and tongue so I don't have to hear her voice again, but that's … wait, what the *hell* am I saying?'

'Katie, think about this carefully,' Dr Chalmers cooed, her hand now pressed gently on top of mine. 'She's a witness.'

'I won't say anything!' Heather pleaded from behind us.

'You won't say anything because in a few hours you're going to be a flesh-eater like the rest of us,' I barked back. 'Now shut the hell up and let the grown-ups talk.'

The sound of incessant gunfire punctuated the dying moans of those still lingering in the gym. Through the high windows set into the gym walls, I could see the reflection of a moving spotlight that was undoubtedly being trained on the school to catch a glimpse of anyone left inside. The other zombies were quiet now, feeding happily on the remains of their classmates. They were in no hurry to leave.

'Security will be closing in,' Dr Chalmers murmured and clasped my hand tightly in hers. 'We need to find another way out of here.'

'We could escape across the oval,' I reasoned, knowing we'd have to negotiate a few well-lit corridors to get there. 'There may be Zone Security surrounding the entire area, but that's a risk we're going to have to take. I very much doubt that they're inspecting wounds before popping lead into the stragglers.'

'And, what about her?'

I looked back at Heather again. She was clutching the wound on her shoulder, but her tear-stained face was resolute. 'I'm coming with you.'

Dr Chalmers frowned. 'Katie—'

'No, she's right. She has to come with us or they'll kill her for sure.'

Dr Chalmers looked displeased but eventually nodded and leapt to her feet. 'Fine. Now how the hell do we get out of this place?'

CHAPTER FOURTEEN

We didn't get out. Zone Security had already begun to stampede their way through the corridors of the school as we were formulating our escape plan. Dr Chalmers, Heather, and I had only a second to glance at each other in fear before we fell to playing our parts. We just hoped we wouldn't get one right between the eyes.

The spotlights reached us before we'd moved a muscle. We sat curled up by the wall, the three of us huddling together and trying to look as victimised as possible. For Heather, that wasn't hard; for Dr Chalmers and I, the urge to flee was almost inbuilt, and our limbs twitched. We gripped each other's hands and prayed that they'd try to contain us rather than kill us outright.

I jumped as Trenton got a bullet right up the ass. He popped up from the cheerleader in surprise and took a fresh one in the temple. He fell to the floor, dead, his vengeful rampage finally over.

Black-clad Zone Security guards fanned out into the room, stopping to execute any zombie they saw feeding. They even put bullets into the dead or dying around us, just to be sure.

We still hadn't moved. We were terrified that our own deaths were imminent.

When security reached the three of us, we were cowering.

Covered in her own blood, Heather was quietly crying, her face ashen. Dr Chalmers and I just held each other.

'This one's injured,' one of them said, flicking the barrel of the gun ever so casually in Heather's direction.

Another guard leaned closer to inspect her but still kept a careful distance. 'She's going to turn. Put her in the cage with the others.'

Heather screamed as they pulled her to her feet, their guns pressed into her spine, and propelled her towards the door of the gym. Crying hysterically, she kept looking back at me, her eyes pleading for help.

'This one has blood on her but no visible wounds. In fact, she may be okay.'

'Put her in the cage, regardless. We won't know who's uninfected until we sift through the wounded.'

I was yanked to my feet but never once protested their brutality as they shoved their gun barrels against my flesh. I took a calming breath and forced myself to comply, knowing that the slightest mistake would see me riddled with bullets.

Dr Chalmers tried to hang onto me, her fingernails tearing at my skin as they dragged me away. 'Katie!' she yelled, strangely frantic now that we were being separated. With my eyes, I begged her to stay calm, but my mild-mannered therapist had begun to scream her discontent and wouldn't quit.

Her howling abruptly stopped, punctuated by a gasping breath as a Zone guard kicked her in the ribs, his rubber boot connecting with enough force to send her flying.

Dr Chalmers made the ultimate mistake—she reared in defence and hissed at her attacker, baring her bloodstained teeth. I turned away as a wave of authority pressed down on her, shouts of horror and then a single gunshot echoing out around the gym.

That gunshot signalled an end to my sessions with Dr Chalmers.

I was ushered quickly through the gym doors and forced to step over a mess of dead and dismembered bodies. My stomach roiled with need, but I managed to force every ounce of instinct down. I was still in a heap of trouble here.

We quickly caught up to Heather's group. She was still sobbing and struggling to catch her breath. I was shoved against her by the two brutish oafs at my side, who prodded us like cattle through the school gates and out into the car park.

I squinted into the bright light of the spotlights trained on us, my vision finally clearing as we were urged towards a number of steel cages that now littered either side of the car park. I could see that most of my surviving classmates were trapped inside them, their collective arms reaching through the bars as they cried out for help.

Heather was suddenly accosted by a group of security intent on touching up her makeup. One of the guards shook a can of red spray paint and fired it full into her face. She cried out as the coloured lacquer seeped into her eyes and mouth; the security guards were merciless, though, and soon after one of their cronies came after me with a can of blue.

Now marked and judged, we were quickly separated. Heather was thrown into a cage with others who were similarly marked, and equally wounded. I was placed in a cage with the blue Smurfs, those others who were free of obvious injury but still under suspicion.

The cries of those afflicted with only minor cuts and abrasions were deafening. Their innocence would be irrelevant come morning, when the others trapped inside with them would turn and fall on their first meals.

Everyone not locked in the cages, or ripped apart in the school corridors beyond, had presumably either gotten away or been shot on sight.

'Palmer!'

I spun around to find Connor crouching behind me. He quickly slipped his arms around my waist, kissing me fiercely. His hands traced their way across my body, seeking out any injury that may have been inflicted since we'd been parted. 'I'm okay,' I said, squeezing his hands tightly in my own. 'Are you?'

He shook his head. 'I can't find my aunt. You were right—she must have circled back around. I can see her car at the edge of the car park, but she's not in any of the cages.'

A couple of other teens pressed up against us, mumbling apologies as they tried to find room elsewhere in the close confines. They looked sad and sorry for themselves. They must have been contemplating their fate and the fate of their friends.

Connor and I moved into the corner, huddling closer for privacy. 'I'm so sorry, Connor, but your aunt didn't make it.'

'What do you mean?'

I hesitated for one shaky breath. 'They guessed what she was and shot her on sight.'

Connor fisted a hand through his hair, a string of tears now running down his cheeks. 'Katie ... she was all I had left.'

'You've got me, Connor. Your aunt made sure of that.'

He didn't say anything then, just buried his face against my shoulder. I couldn't hear him crying but felt him shudder at my touch. I smoothed my hands up and down his spine, conscious of the other students who were doing the same to each other. We'd all lost people we loved tonight.

'We aren't safe,' Connor finally mumbled. He lifted his

head, some of the blue lacquer trailing his tears as they ran down his stained cheeks. 'They've put us in the cages so they can test us.'

'What do you mean? Like a blood test?'

He nodded reluctantly. 'Both of our secrets will be revealed soon enough. We're going to be separated, Palmer. You'll be killed or sent to the desert, and I'll become the subject of some massive government experiment.'

'What can we do?'

'Nothing, Katie. Nothing.'

I didn't have anything useful to add because what Connor had said had rung true—there was no escape this time. We were all destined to be judged and punished accordingly. Those that were lucky enough to be found innocent would be forever haunted by the bloodshed of this night, tormented by visions of those deaths and how close they'd come to it.

As it turned out, Nikki *had* managed to get away, but in her haste to save me she'd torn the flesh from her back escaping the gym door's architrave. Zone Security had cared little for the difference between a bite and a war wound, and had sprayed Nikki's face crimson. I could see her from my own prison, marked and stuck in a cage with those that were turned or turning. I knew if they didn't test them all soon, my best friend would be ripped apart before my eyes.

Blood streaked Nikki's emerald dress, and she cried with the knowledge of her impending death.

As morning approached, some students' concerned parents had started to converge on the school grounds. A whole new type of pandemonium was breaking out as each new pair saw their precious child or children crouching in those cramped cages. There was yelling and screaming, a mere accompaniment to all the tears and self-pity.

Connor and I were wrapped in each other's arms. We watched Nikki in the other cage as she tried to keep moving, the predatory gaze of some of her classmates urging her tired legs to propel her round and round in circles.

Blood had been taken from almost all of us now and the results had started pouring in. Thankfully, they'd worked on the red cage first. I found myself crying out in relief as security began to blow out the brains of those that had started to turn, but not before they'd helped Nikki and a few others out of the cage and into the waiting arms of their terrified parents.

'She's going to be all right,' Connor whispered in my ear, rocking me gently in his arms. 'Nikki's safe now, away from anyone who can hurt her.'

'I just don't understand what went wrong,' I murmured.

'It looks like some of our fellow classmates couldn't contain themselves any longer.'

'And it's that easy,' I said, leaning my head back against his shoulder. 'It takes only a second to lose control.'

'It makes you wonder just how many more like them there are hiding in our town,' Connor mused, kissing the side of my temple.

'They won't let this happen again. I wouldn't be surprised if there's a mandatory blood test every week now for all the survivors.'

Connor tightened his arms around me. 'Who knows … there might be a cure soon?' His voice sounded bitter but I knew that was just the fear talking.

Heather watched us from the other cage. She was crumpled in the corner, her bottom lip trembling, knees pulled tightly to her chest. Her shoulder wound had stopped oozing, and her skin had grown pale and strange. Test results were not required because it was painfully obvious what she was becoming. I hoped I hadn't done her an injustice by letting her live, only to be tortured now in her new life as a zombie.

Shouts of unrest began to rouse Connor and I from our drowsy state. We climbed unsteadily to our feet, turning on the spot to find that Zone Security was now entering our cage. They were pushing those they didn't want aside, ramming their guns into already tender ribs, and kicking others who mewled for escape.

Connor's face dropped at their approach, his knees sagging. I caught him and pulled him upright; he surrendered himself to my embrace. We were defeated, frightened and resigned to our fates.

I could see the nefarious intent sparkling in the lead security officer's eyes. They knew.

'Palmer—'

'You're going to be fine,' I reminded him. 'They're going to want to look after you because you're special. You know you may just end up saving all our lives, Connor.'

'I can't—'

'You have to, because it's happening now.' I planted a hasty kiss on his lips and stepped back, facing the security guards with my hands held out in surrender. There was no point denying the inevitable, especially after those trigger-happy clowns started popping a few rounds in my shoulder. The force of those blasts sent me flying to the ground.

'Move!' one of the security members shouted, pressing the hot barrel of his shotgun against my seeping wound. It was already healing, but the pain was indescribable. My eyes freely watered as the sadistic bastard pulled me back up by my hair.

'Palmer!' Connor tried to rush to my side but was quickly hauled back into the huddle of gunslingers.

'I'm fine,' I gasped, pulling my now-ragged hair from out

of the guard's tight grip. He compensated by grounding the shotgun deeper into the bleeding wound, walking me hurriedly towards the cage's exit. Several guns were focused on me, the faces above each a blur of disgust and grisly resolve.

Panting from the pain, I was herded towards the second cage. It was bursting with writhing flesh-eaters that were hungry for the taste of blood. I wasn't afraid of being consumed, but only that I was destined for the firing line like the others.

I began to weigh up the odds. I studied the trained gunmen around me and wondered if I was as light on my feet as I'd believed. I knew that entertaining the mere idea of escape was ludicrous, but the primal instinct to flee—deeply ingrained within—was rising up in me.

My legs were already propelling me towards a gap in the crowd, towards a cluster of trees, as Connor shouted, 'Palmer, no!'

It was too late. I pumped my legs harder and harder, and had almost, almost, almost made it to the tree line when the first shot rang out. It clipped the side of my ear, spraying an arc of blood across my cheek and forcing me to stumble. The second shot was infinitely more accurate, clipping the back of my thigh and sending me down to the dry dirt below.

I could hear Connor screaming my name over and over again, and though I tried to get up and crawl away, the shots kept on coming. They were like a cracking symphony of death.

The final shot took me to a place of peace. I didn't see it coming and barely heard the cock and release. I felt the press of a shotgun barrel burning against the back of my neck, and then a bullet was passing through flesh and tissue, a dying plea caught in my throat. It ruptured my oesophagus and smashed through my spine.

The world went dark after that, a tiny flicker of light behind my fluttering eyelids the only reminder that I used to be alive, that I used to be Katie Palmer, the diary-writing teenage zombie of Zone Two. Now I was nothing, just a fading pound of flesh that was soon to be forgotten in the hearts and minds of those I'd once known.

I was just Katie Palmer—dead zombie and failed Olympic sprinter.

Fuck.

EPILOGUE

Dear Diary,

It's been a while. So long, in fact, that you probably don't even know me anymore. God only knows what Mum and Dad did with the old version of you, although they probably had a celebratory bonfire in the backyard after reading about my sex life.

Well, obviously I'm not dead. The wanker who put that last round in me left me to bleed out and forgot about the head shot. What an idiot. It's called YouTube!

Anyway, it turns out Zone Security were pretty impressed by my attempted getaway. My tidy ten-second dash to the tree line inspired a whole new wave of zombie hysteria. Zombies like me—relatively fresh and athletically capable—are no longer shipped out to storage facilities in the desert. We're now caged, fed rodents and other sorry excuses for fresh meat, and are shoved in front of the cameras for primetime viewing.

I'm now classed as an Olympic sprinter. It's a dream come true.

Or is it?

With hundreds of weapons trained in my direction every night, I reluctantly race against an eclectic collection of undead competitors all vying to cross the finish line first. If I come last, then one lucky member of the audience has the chance to be the one to blow my brains out.

Now, that's entertainment!

I haven't heard from or seen Connor in months. I know he's still out there, though. His face is on every billboard, sign and t-shirt. He's being hailed as the saviour of our race, the last ray of hope for a population that is slowly dying.

Maybe—one day—we'll get to see each other again, but I doubt it. I just hope the powers that be can get this cure sorted out soon because tomorrow I'm up against some seven-foot Zulus.

Now those fuckers can really run!

Katie xo

COMING SOON FROM KRISTY BERRIDGE...

The Aligned

Volume 3 of
THE HUNTED SERIES

www.ingramcontent.com/pod-product-compliance
Lightning Source LLC
Chambersburg PA
CBHW070624130626
46556CB00001B/466